SEEDS OF REBELLION

The First French and Indian War

Teresa Williams Irvin

HeartChild, Inc.   Langley, Washington

This edition was prepared for publication by
Ghost River Images
5350 East Fourth Street
Tucson, Arizona 85711
www.ghostriverimages.com

ISBN 978-0-9799395-4-9

Library of Congress Control Number: 2013908157

Published in the United States of America

September 2013

Contents

For the Daughters and Sons of the American Revolution who, for generations, have dedicated themselves to the remembrance of our forefathers' passion and sacrifice for this wonderful country, the United States of America—and for readers seeking wisdom and strength from the past.

INTRODUCTION

SEEDS OF WAR

For years England and France, the world's greatest powers, fought each other. In 1748, they reached an uneasy truce—but their struggle for power had spread to the colonies.

The French claimed much of the North American continent. They built forts and settlements from Quebec, Canada south to New Orleans. The English felt they owned the land because John Cabot and his sons had sailed along the coast around 1500—saw it before the French did—and claimed it for England.

Understandably reluctant to give up their ancestral grounds to foreigners, the Indians were a threat from the beginning. The French tried to win them over through trade—especially of furs—and by marrying Indian women and raising families.

The English turned Indian hunting grounds into farms and town sites, broke treaties, and—with some exceptions—generally treated the Indians with contempt. But they offered them better guns and blankets at lower prices and provided them with English rum.

Rugged mountains and almost impenetrable forests made trade difficult in the New World. The best way to transport goods was by water. By the mid-1700s, it was clear that the country in possession of the Ohio and Mississippi Rivers would rule the whole

North American continent. The battle was on between the French and the English to secure it.

As more and more British settlers were willing to brave the terrain and threat of Indians, colonial governments and land speculators came up with a plan to establish land companies to settle the Valley of the Ohio. The most famous of these was the Ohio Company.

In July of 1752 the Marquis Duquesne, head of French expeditionary forces, decided to launch a full-scale military occupation of the Ohio country. Alarmed by reports of Duquesne's troops moving down from Canada, Governor Robert Dinwiddie called the General Assembly of Virginia into session. The decision was made to order the French to leave the Ohio country. George Washington, twenty-one and already a major in the Virginia militia, attended the meeting. Eager to serve his country, he volunteered to ride 500 miles on horseback to carry the message.

Washington arrived at Venango, a stockade cabin in the Ohio country, in December of 1753. He was accompanied by Christopher Gist, a famous scout; an interpreter; four fur traders; and Half King, chief of the Senecas. The French commander at Venango sent them on to Captain Legardeur de Saint-Pierre, the officer stationed at Fort Le Boeuf, almost 100 miles upriver. Hampered by snow, rain, mud, and swamps, Washington's party struggled for four days to get there.

Washington delivered Governor Dinwiddie's letter demanding the "peaceful departure" of the French from the Ohio. Saint-Pierre rejected the ultimatum, and Washington returned to Williamsburg, Virginia's colonial capitol.

Meanwhile, the Ohio Company had hired frontiersmen to start work on a fortified post at the forks of the Ohio River to protect the settlers in the valley. Although not completed, it was named Fort Prince George in honor of England's future king.

Governor Dinwiddie promoted Washington to Colonel and ordered him to enlist 100 men to march to Fort Prince George—a task that proved to be difficult. Recruits and wagons to move provisions and equipment were hard to come by. Most colonists on the East Coast seemed unconcerned about what was happening to settlers in the backcountry.

Washington was marching his men to Fort Prince George when a courier arrived and informed him that 500 French troops and Indians under the command of Captain Claude Contrecoeur had arrived at the fort and demanded its surrender. Outnumbered, the English complied. Fort Prince George was now Fort Duquesne.

Terrified settlers and traders straggled into Washington's camp with tales of atrocities committed by the French and their Indian allies. Washington decided to push on, await reinforcements, and retake the fort. He and his men were camped in a valley called Great Meadows when Washington received word that French soldiers were marching out from Fort Duquesne to meet them.

Contrecour had sent Coulon de Jumonville, a young ensign from an illustrious French family, with a small detachment to Great Meadows to present Washington with a "summons," asking him to depart from what they considered to be French territory or face the consequences.

Convinced that Jumonville was going to attack, Washington and his men, accompanied by Half King and others of his Seneca tribe, surrounded the French detachment when they halted for the night and attacked them at dawn. During the battle Half King discovered Jumonville wounded, crushed the ensign's skull with his tomahawk, and washed his hands with his brains.

The only French soldier to escape returned to Fort Duquesne and recounted how Jumonville's peaceful mission had been met with an unwarranted attack—a story that became widely publicized in France.

Washington retreated to Great Meadows—where, in five days' time, his weary, hungry men constructed a wretched fort they named Fort Necessity. Half King and his scouts deserted. There was little to eat but flour.

As Washington expected, the French did not let Jumonville's death go unavenged. Captain Coulon de Villiers marched his men to Fort Necessity. There, a bloody battle took place under a

7

violent downpour. One third of Washington's men were killed or wounded. Having no other option, he accepted Villiers' conditions for surrender.

Most of the Articles of Capitulation were reasonable, but one item would haunt Washington the rest of his life. Unable to read some of the rain-spattered document, his interpreter failed to see the word l'assassin. Washington had signed a confession admitting he was an assassin.

Governor Dinwiddie renewed his pleas to the Crown for assistance and put out a call for men to march back across the mountains and retake Fort Duquesne. The British Parliament finally voted to send Major General Edward Braddock to the colonies with two Irish regiments to help the Americans defeat the French and remove their threat to take over the continent.

AUTHOR'S NOTE

Although Josh Bedford, his family, and some of his friends are fictional characters, many of the others are not, including George Washington, Daniel Boone, Half King, and Bright Lightning. The attack on Lettie Martin's family was inspired by the following letter, written by my great, great, great, great grandmother, Elizabeth Marshall Martin:

Plantation

June thirteen, 1755

Dear Brother Thomas:

We are in much confusion and distress because of the burning of our out houses last night. They have taken away every horse and fowl and soon after they left the barnes were found to be burning. They did not come to the house and I do not think they were the Indians. Gen Braddock and staff camped here several nights ago. He informed father Martin that Abram had taken his command to join Col Washington with General Braddock on their way to Ft Duquesne. I would it were so that you and Mary could come here for awhile. Two of the children have measles and father Martin is sick with dysentery and I am in bed with a baby three days old and am too weak to get up. I fear the return of the enemy. Do come if possible. We have no horse to send for you. David will take this to you. I have brought the blacks into the house. We have two guns.

Your affectionate Sister
Elizabeth.

The baby mentioned was John Marshall, the fourth Chief Justice of the United States and acknowledged Father of our American Judicial System.

CHAPTER ONE

TROUBLE

A noise outside the cabin yanked me awake. No light yet through the window. The sun wasn't up. I held my breath and listened.

"Hello, the cabin!" a gruff voice shouted.

I nudged my brother, asleep on the pallet beside me, and scrambled to my feet.

"Wh-what is it?" Matt mumbled.

"Something's happened!" I peeled off my nightshirt—then grabbed my shirt and breeches off a peg and pulled them on as a candle in the room below flickered and steadied, casting shadows on the split-log walls. Matt followed me down the ladder to the ground floor.

Pa threw the latch and opened the cabin door, his longrifle at the ready. He peered at the face of the bearded man panting on the threshold. "Ben! What brings you out so early in the morning?"

I recognized Mister Mason at once. He stopped by every now and then when he checked his traps.

"Somethin' terrible's happened," he gasped.

"Come in," Pa said.

Mister Mason was limping. Pa helped him to a chair while Matt closed the door and set the latch.

"Here, rest yourself and tell us about it." Pa sat down and glanced at Ma, who was already stoking the fire to heat the kettle for tea.

Mister Mason caught his breath. "Injuns hit the Gregorson's place," he said in a low voice.

I shivered. The Gregorson's farm was only four miles away!

"What of the family?" Pa asked.

Mister Mason shook his head. "Murdered. All three of 'em."

I couldn't believe it. Only last week they had brought their baby by to visit.

Ma stifled a cry.

"Damn bloody savages," Mister Mason muttered "—beggin' your pardon Miz Bedford."

Pa leaned forward in his chair. "What happened, Ben?"

"Sam Gregorson invited me to sup and spend the night." He stared at the fire. "I was up in the loft. Next thing I knowed, there's a shot fired. The baby started to cry—then Miz Gregorson screamed." Mister Mason rubbed his eyes with the palms of his hands. "Time I grabbed my rifle it was all over—all of 'em dead and the cabin burnin'. I jumped out the window and hid in the woods." He rubbed his leg. "Them Injuns was so busy scalpin' and lootin', they never seen me."

I felt sick.

"The cabin burned?" Pa asked.

Mister Mason nodded. "Nothin' left to bury."

"Josh?" Pa turned and looked at me.

I pretended not to hear. My little sister Sarah toddled in, whimpering, from the bedroom. Ma scooped her up and shushed her.

"It's almost daylight," Pa said. "Time to tend to the cow, Josh."

"Now, Pa?" He wanted me to milk the cow while Matt got to stay and hear the whole story? I gave him a pleading look, but he ignored it.

"Now."

Ma frowned. "Is it safe for him to leave the cabin, James?"

"The raiding party that attacked the Gregorsons will be enjoying their spoils. He'll be fine."

Matt turned so that only I could see his grin. Scowling, I made for the door and ran down the path to the barn, the air of early May cold on my cheeks. A sharp stick ripped through my moccasin! I grabbed my hurt foot and plunked down in the weeds. Why was it my chore to milk Bessy twice a day, anyhow, I fumed. Why not Matt? Just because he was older? We could at least take turns. It wasn't fair! But Matt was Pa's favorite. Always had been.

I squeezed back tears. Matt thought he was so great—bragging all the time about the things he was going to do. Now he was talking about leaving home and joining the rangers! He'd gotten worse since he turned fifteen. I got even, though. I was taller than him by inches. He hated that.

Matt and I tangled every single day. Like last night, after I brought in the milk. He was showing off his new sling. He let me try it out, and the darn thing broke! He picked a fight. Ma had to break it up. Pa blamed me, of course—but it wasn't my fault. The leather Matt used to make the dang sling was too thin. How was I to know that?

I took off my moccasin and inspected my arch—almost disappointed the stick hadn't punctured the skin. Then they'd be sorry. At least Ma would. I slipped the moccasin on again and limped toward the barn.

The barn door was open! I started to run, in spite of my foot. "Bessy!" I cried. "Bessy!" I peered inside the gloomy barn, praying to see her in the shadows. The barn was empty. The cow was gone. Indians! I glanced around, my heart beating fast—but everything looked the same as always. What had I done last night? I racked my brain, trying to remember every detail. I had finished milking, set the milking stool aside, picked up the bucket of milk—then walked outside and latched the barn door behind me to take the milk to the cabin. I did latch it. Didn't I? A guilty feeling settled in the pit of my stomach. The cow couldn't have gotten out, if I'd truly dropped the latch in place.

I closed the barn door and latched it—then slowly walked to

the cabin. Facing Pa would be hard enough. The thought of Matt listening and secretly gloating was worse.

Sarah sat beside the open doorway playing with Cinder, our family cat. My sister had suffered a fever, and in the dawning sunlight her face looked pale and thin. A pang of fear shot through me. She needed milk to get her strength back. I had to find the cow—and quickly.

The shutters we closed at night for protection had been opened. Pa was still in his chair beside the kitchen table. "Better let my wife have a look at that, Ben," he said.

Mister Mason eyed his ankle. "Naw, it's all right."

I moved closer to the door—then paused, trying to screw up my courage.

"Colonel Washington's mission to the Ohio Valley last year really riled them French and their Injuns," Mister Mason grumbled. "We never had trouble like this before."

I was about to die with my news about the cow, and they were talking politics! Just a few more seconds…

Pa grunted. "The governor should have sent someone older and more experienced than Washington to deal with the French."

I couldn't wait any longer. I moved to the doorway, swallowing hard to try and get rid of the lump in my throat. Cinder escaped Sarah's hugs as she moved aside to let me pass.

"Milk, Joshie?"

"Bessy's gone," I muttered. The heavy lid Ma had lifted to inspect the porridge clattered into place.

Matt had been fiddling with his sling. He stuck it in his belt and looked at me—hesitated—then pointed at the empty milk pail. "Josh says Bessy's gone, Pa."

I straightened to my full height and looked down on him.

Pa leaped to his feet. "Where is Bessy, Joshua?" He only called me Joshua when he was really angry. "What did you do this time— or more likely, what didn't you do?"

"What happened, Josh?" The look on Ma's face was hard to take.

14

"I'll tell you what happened," Pa roared, before I could answer. "He didn't latch the barn door!"

I saw Matt's lips curl with satisfaction.

"Did you, Joshua?" Pa said.

"I latched it, Pa," I tried to convince him, but I couldn't meet his eye.

Mister Mason cleared his throat and shoved his chair back from the table. "Thanks fer your hospitality, Miz Bedford."

Shamed and embarrassed, I watched him get up and limp away.

"Sorry, Ben," Pa called after him. Turning, he glared at me and motioned to Matt. "C'mon, son. Let's see if we can find the cow before something happens to her."

Would Pa ever call me son like that? "Take me with you," I pleaded. "I know Bessy better than anybody and I'm a good tracker."

Pa reached for his longrifle. "You stay with Sarah and your mother. I'll deal with you later."

Matt grinned and swung through the door after Pa, his own longrifle tucked under his arm. I watched them disappear into the woods together.

"I could've helped, Ma."

She wiped her hands on her apron—then sighed and turned back to the fireplace. "Your father's worried."

No need to tell me that. My stomach twisted at the sight of Sarah's skinny arms.

The minutes stretched into what seemed like hours, and Pa and Matt didn't return. I cleaned out the barn, hoping Pa would notice when he came home. I swept Bessy's stall and hauled the dung to dry beside Ma's vegetable garden—then rinsed the cow's trough in the creek and filled it with fresh water, trying to convince myself that Bessy would be back to drink it. Every little while I stopped what I was doing and strained to listen for Pa's return, but the only break in the silence was the buzzing of a pesky horsefly.

I reached into the hayrack, scooping up armloads of hay and dropping them into Bessy's feedbox. Suddenly, instead of hay, my fingers curled around a long hard object. A longrifle! I had over-heard my parents discuss the possibility of giving me one for my birthday. In just seventy-six more days, I'd be fourteen. I'd been counting the days for months.

I stroked the wooden stock and ran my fingers down the barrel. The gun was five feet long—some eight inches shorter than me. I had dreamed of owning such a weapon.

"Joshua!"

Pa! I shoved the rifle deep into the hay again and ran out of the barn toward the cabin.

"The cow's dead," Pa's words floated through the open door-way.

"Indians killed her," Matt said.

Ma frowned. "Indians came that close to the farm? But James, you said they wouldn't..."

Pa interrupted her. "They must have been hungry. They butch-ered the cow."

"Took most everything but the bones," Matt said.

"Where's Joshua?" Pa asked.

I braced myself to face him.

"There he is!" Matt pointed to my shadow on the threshold.

Pa spun around, his eyes blazing.

"Please, James—don't!" Ma cried. Sarah buried her face in Ma's skirt and began to wail.

Matt gave me a smug look as Pa stalked to the bedroom and reached for the willow switch propped in the corner behind the door. Minutes later he had me bent over the hayrack, my breeches around my feet while the switch whined its way to my bare legs.

I couldn't eat the gingerbread Ma baked for supper—even though I knew she'd cooked it to try and cheer me up.

"Eat it," Pa said, scowling. "Your mother went to a lot of trouble to fix it."

I clenched my teeth and stared at the wall.

"Well then, you'd best leave."

16

I got up from the table—couldn't look at Ma—and climbed the wooden ladder to the loft. There I peeled off my shirt and breeches and hung them on a peg. I put on my nightshirt—then eased my bruised legs onto the straw tick pallet I shared with Matt and stretched out.

The evening star winked at me through the window. What could I wish for? There was no bringing Bessy back—that was for sure. Pa asked me to leave, meaning the table. I wished I could leave home, but where would I go and what would I do? If there was a town close-by, things might be different. Here in the wilderness... I was trapped. Thoughts of Bessy... Sarah... the longrifle... tumbled through my mind and I fell asleep—until Pa slapped the table in the room below with the palm of his hand. Wide awake, I pressed my ear to the knothole in the floor I used when I wanted to eavesdrop and listened.

"There's no need to curse, James," Ma said. "Josh will be fourteen this July. He wants a longrifle more than anything. You gave Matt his gun when he turned fourteen."

"Matt's a responsible lad. I was wrong to buy that longrifle for Josh. He hasn't earned it. I've told him a hundred times to be careful. It was bad enough when he let the pigs out and we lost the shoat. Now this."

I strained to hear Ma's answer.

"Josh tries—really he does."

"But he doesn't listen. Half the time, he doesn't tell the truth. And you protect him."

I peered through the knothole and saw Ma pick up her sewing. "You're probably right, but after we lost little Jed, I couldn't help it."

My brother Jed died when we were babies. I'd often wondered what it would be like, having a twin. Ma said Jed and I were alike as two peas. Would he be tall now, with gray eyes and curly blonde hair? Would Pa like him better than he liked me? I sighed, wishing I'd been the one who died.

"If it hadn't been for the Indians, you would have found the cow," Ma said.

Pa snorted. "Blasted savages grow bolder every day."

I stopped listening and dozed until I heard Pa mention my name again.

"If only Josh was more like Matt."

I looked at my brother snoring beside me and consoled myself with the thought that the breeches I'd outgrown—that Ma was now patching because I had torn them climbing a tree—would soon be his to wear.

"Matt's been a good boy," Ma said. "Very reliable."

Ma! I pressed my ear closer to the floor, so as not to miss anything else she might have to say, but she changed the subject.

"All children aren't the same, James. Look at your own brother. You're different as day and night."

"Harry," Pa grunted.

Uncle Harry was a corporal with the Virginia Militia, had served under Colonel Washington last year at Fort Necessity. For as long as I could remember, I had dreamed of following in his footsteps. No old farm for Uncle Harry. He fought real people, not limestone boulders and tree stumps in the fields, like Pa. The two men hardly even looked like brothers. Uncle Harry was as tall and muscular as Pa was short and thin. When Grandmother Bedford was alive, she used to talk about how much everybody liked Uncle Harry. Why didn't Pa like him? It wasn't Uncle Harry's fault—that was for sure.

Pa's voice droned on. "Point is, Sarah has to have milk if she's to regain her strength. I don't have to tell you how frail she is. We were lucky not to lose her last month."

I thought about the three small graves in the family cemetery: two sisters and Jed, who had died of fever. Ma visited their graves every Sunday.

"We need another cow," Pa said. "That's all there is to it. Short as we are of cash, I'll have to sell the gun—or maybe Amos will trade me for it."

Amos Porter was our closest neighbor. It was settled, then. The rifle—the beautiful longrifle—wasn't mine, after all. The tears I'd managed to hold back all day burned my cheeks and melted into the pillow. I rubbed them away; glad Matt wasn't awake to see.

CHAPTER TWO

UNCLE HARRY

Rain drumming on the roof wakened me next morning. The air in the loft smelled damp and stale. I rolled over on the pallet, nagged by the thought that something was wrong. Then I remembered. Bessy... I stared at a chink in the wall. What was it Ma always said? Groaning, I remembered. "No use crying over spilt milk." Matt was already gone. I took off my nightshirt and pulled on my clothes—then climbed down the ladder to face the family. Cinder greeted me with a meow and rubbed against my legs. Pa and Matt ignored me. They were sitting on a bench against the wall cleaning their longrifles. I picked up the pitcher, poured water in the bowl on the washstand, and washed my face.

Ma reached into the fireplace for the steaming porridge. Glad of something to do, I motioned her aside and lifted the pot from its iron hook.

"Careful," she whispered.

Too late. The porridge sloshed on the table when I plunked it down. I could feel my face turn red. I looked at Pa and Matt to see if they'd noticed, while Ma hurried to clean up the mess. Matt had noticed, all right. He grinned and mouthed the words, "Mama's boy."

We sat down at the table and bowed our heads. Pa said grace, thanking the Almighty for all His blessings and beseeching Him to lead me, in particular, "down the path of righteousness." Matt kicked me on the shin and grinned. I flashed him a dirty look and showed him my fist.

"Amen," Pa said at last.

There were no warm biscuits this morning. No milk, I thought, feeling guilty. Ma served up what was left of yesterday's batch. I managed a smile. "Thanks, Ma." Without cream the porridge was thick and tasteless.

"Sh!" Pa held up a hand for quiet.

Through the sound of the rain, I could hear the rumble of a wagon. Two visitors in two days? That hardly ever happened.

Pa snatched up his longrifle. Moving to the door, he opened the peephole as a familiar voice called out, "Open up, James—it's me, your brother."

Pa lifted the latch and the door swung open. Uncle Harry grabbed him in a bear hug, the strings on his buckskin tunic dripping. "You're a sight for sore eyes, James—and you, Grace—I'll swear, but you're prettier every time I see you." He laughed.

Ma looked away, her face pink. She didn't seem to notice the mud he had tracked in on her clean floor.

It was like a fresh wind had blown through the cabin. When Uncle Harry hugged me I hugged him back, hard as I could—sniffing the wonderful smells of leather and tobacco that always clung to him. Matt looked sideways at Pa and tried to keep his distance. Uncle Harry paid no attention and hugged him anyway

Sarah woke up and whimpered. I hurried to the bedroom to get her. Shy when she saw Uncle Harry, she ducked her face against my shirt. He winked and grinned. Digging in his pouch, he pulled out a chunk of rock candy and held it out. I set her down, and she went right to him.

Uncle Harry sank into a chair beside the kitchen table, Sarah in his lap sucking her treat while Ma lifted the kettle from the fire to make tea.

"Sorry, but we haven't any milk," she murmured as she set his cup on the table.

"Josh let the cow get out and Indians killed her." Matt said.

"No problem." Uncle Harry smiled and reached inside his pouch again. "I've got something better than milk." Pulling out a flask, he offered some rum to Pa. Pa shook his head, and I saw him and Ma exchange a disapproving look.

"What're you doing here, Harry?" Pa asked.

"The Crown finally came through with reinforcements to help us retake Fort Duquesne."

Redcoats, here in Virginia! The thought thrilled me.

Pa snorted. "About time."

"The militia's at Fort Cumberland, waiting for them."

"How many men did the king send?"

"Two regiments, commanded by General Braddock."

"I've heard of Braddock. He has a good reputation."

Uncle Harry shrugged. "Maybe so—in England. Folks here in the colonies find him ill-tempered and arrogant."

Pa bit his lip—a sure sign he wanted to say something and was holding back. Finally, he said, "How many troops, altogether?"

"With Indians and special detachments, around two thousand."

"What Indians?"

"Half King and his scouts." Uncle Harry chuckled. "Washington's been beating the bushes, trying to come up with recruits—says he could as easily have raised the dead as a company of Virginians to fight this battle."

"Washington!" Pa sneered. "I thought he resigned his commission after the rout at Fort Necessity."

Uncle Harry had fought beside Colonel Washington at Fort Necessity and shared his bitter defeat. Appalled by what Pa said and the tone of his voice when he said it, I listened for Uncle Harry's response.

Uncle Harry just looked at Pa—then slowly choosing his words answered, "When the king decided to send us an army, James, he stipulated that our officers would be subordinate to his, and no colonist could hold a rank above that of captain. Washington was a colonel in the militia, as you no doubt recall. He resigned, rather than submit to the king's orders." Uncle Harry glanced at Ma and his voice lost its edge. "Braddock talked him into coming back into service as his aide."

Anxious to break the tension, I risked Pa's anger by changing the subject. "Where's your uniform, Uncle Harry?"

"This is it." He touched his buckskin tunic. His breeches, moccasins, and gaiters were also made out of buckskin. "Washington said we enlisted men could wear regular clothes. They're cheaper than uniforms and a lot more practical."

Practical or not, I was disappointed.

Uncle Harry smiled. "British uniforms look good on a parade ground, Josh—but those red coats also make fine targets."

Pa reached for his pipe and Uncle Harry pulled one out of his pouch. I hurried to the fireplace for a spill to light them while they filled them with tobacco.

Uncle Harry puffed on his pipe and exhaled a stream of smoke. "Colonel Dunbar's 48th Regiment should arrive at Fort Cumberland tomorrow. The general's with him. We expect Halkett's 44th next week." He took a swallow of his rum-laced tea. "One of Dunbar's scouts visited us last night. He said the 48th is camped at Cresap's plantation."

"Cresap!" Pa snarled. "He's a vile rascal!"

Uncle Harry nodded. "I don't know what he did to you, but he sold the army un-pickled beef and it spoiled immediately. The men couldn't bury it fast enough."

Cinder leaped into Uncle Harry's lap and settled in next to Sarah. Instead of brushing him away as Pa would have done, Uncle Harry reached down and rubbed his ears. "That's one reason I'm here, James. I'm on the hunt for supplies. Is there anything you can let us have?"

Pa thought a minute. "There's a hogshead of tobacco in the shed ready to ship."

If Pa sold the tobacco, maybe he'd change his mind about the longrifle!

"Matt and I have to go to Porters' today to trade for a new cow,"

Pa said. "I'll see what Amos has."

A feeling of loss swept over me.

"I was going to ask the boys if they'd like to come with me," Uncle Harry said. "I'm not very familiar with the area. Thought they might show me around. If Matt's busy, maybe Josh could come."

"Oh yes, Pa—please," I said, ignoring Matt's venomous look.

"Well, if you really need him," Pa reluctantly agreed. "But watch out, Harry. I haven't told you… our neighbors were murdered last night."

Uncle Harry's eyes narrowed. "Indians?"

Pa nodded. "Probably Shawnee. They've sided with the French."

"I'll keep my eyes open."

"All right, then." Turning to me, Pa said, "Take him to Martin Plantation."

I'd get to see Lettie! Although we were best friends, we hadn't seen each other for months.

Uncle Harry swallowed the last of his tea and stood up. "The Conestoga's out front, Josh. I'll wait for you."

A Conestoga! I raced up the ladder, grabbed my sling and knife, slipped downstairs again two rungs at a time, and slammed the cabin door behind me. The rain had stopped. Matt and Pa were walking around the wagon while Ma and Sarah watched.

"This the first time you've seen a Conestoga, James?" Uncle Harry asked.

Pa grudgingly admitted that it was.

The wagon was huge. Four bows of bent hickory supported the canvas. I whistled under my breath, looking at the curved side panels sweeping upward front and back on both sides of the wagon bed. The running gear was different from any I'd seen. The wheels at the back were bigger than the ones in front.

Four sturdy draft horses stood waiting in harness. They were at least eighteen hands high—from the look of them, crosses between standard stallions and Clydesdales. It was a good thing they were sound. The wagon was heavy.

"Where'd you get it, Harry?" Pa asked.

"The Pennsylvanians who were supposed to supply wagons and pack horses for the campaign came through with only a fraction of what Braddock expected. Ben Franklin threatened them—said if they didn't make up the difference, they'd be pressed into service. Wagons have been pouring in all week. This is one of them." He swung into the driver's seat.

I started to hug Ma goodbye and changed my mind, still rankling over what she had said about Matt being so dang reliable. Seated beside Uncle Harry, I waited until Pa was inspecting something on the wagon—then looked Matt in the eye and stuck out my tongue.

My spirits improved with every clop of the horses' hooves taking me away from the farm. Uncle Harry glanced at me a couple of times, but he didn't say anything, so I didn't either—until we came to a fork in the trail. "Martins' place is that way." I pointed to the right.

Uncle Harry brought the team to a sudden halt.

Indians? My heart pounded. After what happened to the Gregorsons...

"Why don't you drive?" He handed me the reins.

I caught my breath, trying not to show how relieved I was. Pa never let me drive the wagon like he did Matt. I didn't have any experience, but I wasn't going to tell Uncle Harry that. Besides, I'd watched enough, I ought to be able to do it. I clicked my tongue and flipped the reins over the horses' backs. The team fell into step as if I drove them every day.

We rode through the hills in friendly silence, lulled by the squeak of the wagon wheels. I could feel myself relax. The rain-washed forest was peaceful, the hickories and sweet gum trees covered with spring leaves. Here and there, I could see wildflowers.

Something rustled in the laurel slick lining the road. From the corner of my eye I saw Uncle Harry turn his head and finger the trigger of his longrifle as a covey of quail took flight with a rush of wings. He cradled his gun in the crook of his arm again. "A lot of game around here."

I nodded. "Matt got chased by a buffalo last month. You should've seen him run!" I grinned, remembering.

Uncle Harry chuckled. "I wouldn't let Matt get my goat, if I was you."

"Sir?"

"I said I wouldn't let Matt get under my skin. I see the way you two look at each other."

"Matt thinks he knows everything."

"He'll never be as smart again as he is right now. Believe me, I know what I'm talking about."

"How do you know about Matt and me?"

"It was the same way with me and your pa."

That must be the reason for the problem between Uncle Harry and Pa. I was surprised I hadn't thought of it before. "Pa's almost two years older'n you, isn't he?"

"And he still doesn't like me much." Uncle Harry shrugged. "It doesn't matter. You don't have to like a person in order to love him."

Riding along, I thought about what Uncle Harry said. Did I love Pa? I sure didn't like him sometimes—but I wanted him to show me that he loved me. What about Matt? Did I love him, even when I couldn't stand him? If Matt loved me, he wouldn't pick on me all the time.

Something about our last fight bothered me, but I couldn't figure out what it was. I replayed the whole thing again in my mind. Matt snatched his broken sling away from me and started the fight. Ma broke it up, and Pa blamed me. But then something else happened. What was it?

I searched my mind, trying to remember. Then it came to me. After I milked Bessy, I saw Matt walk toward the barn. The sling was in his hand. He must have gone there to look for a piece of rawhide to replace the thong I broke—because I saw him stick the sling in his belt when I told Pa that Bessy was gone. Matt was the last one in the barn yesterday. Losing the cow wasn't my fault! Relief flooded through me. Good old reliable Matt had let me take the blame.

Rage over what he had done nearly took my breath away. I looked at Uncle Harry, the story of Matt's betrayal on the tip of my tongue—then realized that just telling on Matt wouldn't be enough. Some day... some how... I'd have my revenge.

The team grunted as they pulled the wagon toward the top of the ridge overlooking Martin Plantation. I clicked my tongue, urging them to hurry. Lettie was going to be impressed, when I came in driving a Conestoga.

Suddenly, my nose tingled. Smoke!

CHAPTER THREE

LETTIE

Lettie's house was still standing, but the slave quarters, tobacco shed, barns, smokehouse, smithy and soap house—all the plantation outbuildings had burned. Curls of wispy smoke still rose from the smoldering timbers. I thrust Uncle Harry the reins and jumped out of the wagon. Running down the hill, I heard the whip crack behind me and his command to "Gee!" sending the horses into a gallop.

Lettie! She might be hurt—or worse! And what about her younger brothers—Barclay, and Jake and Jesse the twins, and little Marshall who was Sarah's age—or Mister and Miz Martin, who had always been so good to me? I pounded on the front door.

The door cracked open. The barrel of a longrifle slipped through—aimed at my heart.

"It's me, Josh Bedford! Let me in!"

"Josh!" Lettie swung the door open. Barclay stood beside her.

"Haw!" The horses turned, and Uncle Harry brought them to a halt in front of the house. He leaped from the wagon, his longrifle in hand.

I introduced him.

"You all right?" he asked.

"Yes, sir," Lettie said. "Please, come in."

She and Barclay moved aside to let us pass. I looked around and

29

breathed a sigh of relief that the house had been spared. I couldn't see any damage.

"Where's your father?" Uncle Harry asked.

"With the militia," Lettie answered. "We're not sure where he is."

"And your mother?"

"Mama's in bed. She had a baby and can't get up yet."

I was speechless. This wasn't the Lettie I remembered. She was taller than she used to be and seemed so grown up. But that wasn't all. Her mop of black hair and startling blue eyes I used to tease her about weren't so strange looking any more. She had a blue dress on that looked nice with her eyes, even though her dress and apron were smudged with ashes. I was struck with the thought she was downright pretty.

"Grandfather Martin's staying with us while Papa's gone," Barclay said.

Lettie propped her gun against the wall and motioned to her brother to do the same. "Grandfather's sick with dysentery. I'll see if he's up to company."

Uncle Harry shook his head. "Seems to me your plate's pretty full, young lady."

Lettie's eyes swam with tears, but her voice was firm. "Don't worry about me, sir. I'm fine."

Just then, an old man shuffled into the room. Close as I was to the family, I'd never met Lettie's grandfather. He looked frail, reminding me of Sarah since her illness. His hair was gray, what there was of it—but his blue eyes—which were a lot like Lettie's, were alert as he looked at Uncle Harry and me.

Lettie hurried to his side. "Grandfather, this is Mister—er—Corporal Bedford."

"Harrison Bedford, at your service—and this is my nephew, Josh." Uncle Harry helped Lettie assist Mister Martin into a chair. "You shouldn't have gotten out of bed, sir."

Mister Martin brushed the thought aside. "Have you any news of the Virginia Militia? My son, Abram, is a captain. He has to know

30

what happened here." He sighed, as if too weary to say any more.

"Mama sent a note to Uncle Thomas this morning with our black, David, asking him to try and find Papa," Lettie said, "but Aunt Mary's going to have a baby. We're not sure he'll leave her."

"The militia's assembling at Fort Cumberland," Uncle Harry said. "I'm going back to the fort tomorrow. I'll be more than glad to take your son the message."

"Be grateful, if you would." Groaning, Mister Martin shifted in his chair.

"Who attacked you, do you know?" Uncle Harry asked.

"It was dark, and we couldn't see—but we think it was savages."

Lettie came to the table with some pungent-smelling tea. "This has herbs in it, Grandfather. They'll give you strength."

I tried to catch her eye, but she would hardly look at me. For the first time ever, she made me feel uncomfortable. She walked to the cupboard and began pulling out food.

Mister Martin sipped his tea and looked at Uncle Harry. "We were fortunate in some respects."

"How's that, sir?"

"The slaves escaped injury, and the rain helped to put out the fires." He watched as Lettie set out platters of cold cornbread and cured ham and a bowl of salad greens. "That's enough about our situation. What brings you here?"

"I'm buying supplies for the army. My brother James thought your son might have something to sell."

"We did have some sacks of dry corn, but they were stolen—along with the horses and fowl." Mister Martin motioned to the food. "Please, help yourselves."

I filled my plate and turned to Lettie, seated beside me. She still wouldn't look at me. Finally I whispered, "What's going on with you, anyhow?" so the others couldn't hear.

"What's going on with you?" she whispered back. "You're not acting like yourself at all!"

"I don't know. I can't explain it. You're so... different."

31

She looked at me then. "So are you. You're so tall!"

We were finally able to talk. She told me the twins were down with the measles and that Marshall was asleep. She said the new baby was a boy and then she asked, "How's Matt?"

"Same as always." I wanted to tell her how he had betrayed me, but Lettie had enough troubles of her own right now. "How's our fort?" I whispered.

The fort was a shallow cave the two of us discovered when we were out in the woods hunting blackberries. It was our special place, away from Matt and the others. A creek ran nearby, flowing with clear water that spilled into a deep pool lined with ferns.

"The f-fort?" Her skin turned red all the way up into her hair.

Why was Lettie blushing? I was the one who was embarrassed the last time we were there. It had been a hot summer afternoon. We'd been playing hide and seek with the other kids and were tired of them—especially Matt, with his teasing and lording it over everybody. The last time we were supposed to hide, Lettie and I secretly left and went to the fort. As soon as we got there, she started to take off her clothes.

"What're you doing?" I'd said.

"C'mon, silly," she taunted. "What're you afraid of? It's only water."

"You're a girl and I'm a boy…"

"What does that have to do with anything? I've got brothers!"

"But we're not related! What if we're caught?"

There'd been a flash of bare skin as Lettie plunged into the water.

I was afraid to look at her, at first. Then she ducked me, and I forgot all about her being naked.

Putting on our clothes afterwards, I said, "We have to get these wet."

"Why?" Lettie asked.

"It's late. I'll be leaving with the folks to get back to the farm before dark. Our hair won't have time to dry—especially yours. Our mothers will want to know what happened."

When we arrived back at the cabin Ma and Miz Martin had looked at us curiously and asked a lot of questions. I told them Lettie's berry basket had fallen in the pool and we got wet fishing it out.

Now, sitting beside her, I darted a look at Lettie's amazingly rounded breasts and glanced away, tantalized by the thought of playing in the water with her again.

"Mama's calling." She jumped up from the table and left the room.

I turned my attention to the others as Uncle Harry said, "Braddock told Ben Franklin the capture of Fort Duquesne shouldn't take him more than three or four days. I'm not so sure. The British have the training, all right—but for a different kind of fighting than we're used to."

Mister Martin pushed his chair away from the table. "I must go to my room. Nice to have met you, Harry—and good luck."

Uncle Harry helped him to his feet. "And to you, sir. Hope you're better soon. Don't worry about your son getting the message. If he's at Fort Cumberland, I'll find him." He watched Mister Martin shuffle away and turned to me. "We'd better be on our way."

I looked around for Lettie.

"She must be with Mama," Barclay said.

I walked with Uncle Harry to the door. Barclay came outside with us. "That's some outfit," he said as soon as he saw the wagon.

Uncle Harry swung into place while I climbed up beside him and picked up the reins. "It's a Conestoga."

Where was Lettie? She was the one I really wanted to show the wagon to. Just then she came running, pressed something into my hand, and disappeared. A rose! What in the world had gotten into her?

Uncle Harry eyed it and grinned from ear to ear. "The first rose of spring," he said.

I opened my pouch and dropped it inside, my face burning. Then I released the brake and signaled the team to move.

When we reached the top of the ridge, I looked back. A field behind the burned-out smokehouse had been planted with tobacco. The plants looked healthy in their mounds of rich black mulch. If they hadn't been transplanted, they would have burned along with everything else in the tobacco shed.

I kept up the pace of the horses, my mind on Lettie. Why did she give me that rose? I smiled, thinking about how she had changed. We'd always been friends, but this was different.

The sun began to set, deepening the forest shadows. Raucous Blue Jays cried out to one another as they swooped from tree to tree filled with chirping birds settling down for the night. I was aware of Uncle Harry beside me, his body tense and his eyes watchful as he peered into the dense vegetation on either side of the road. Used to be—the Indians in this area would steal a head or two of livestock and disappear. Not any more.

Uncle Harry would be leaving tomorrow. I hated the idea of seeing him go. He was a grown man who treated me like an equal—and he was going to war. I thought about Pa and Matt... one problem after another, and for the first time in a long time I knew exactly what I wanted to do.

Pa and Matt were outside, waiting for us, when we wheeled up to the cabin. I pulled the team to a halt and set the brake. Pa didn't seem to notice that I had been driving the Conestoga, but Matt sure did. Stepping forward to take hold of the horses' harness, he gave me a hateful look. I jumped down from the wagon and sauntered past him.

Standing beside the wagon, Pa looked up at Uncle Harry. "Did the Martins have any supplies?"

"They were attacked last night. Lost everything but the house." Uncle Harry climbed down to join him.

Pa motioned to Matt. "Take the wagon to the barn, son. Set out fresh feed and water and rub down the horses."

I followed Pa and Uncle Harry to the cabin. Ma was beside the fireplace, as usual.

"Martin's place was burned," Pa said.

"Oh, no!" Her hand flew to her mouth. "How are they?"

"They lost all the outbuildings, but they're all right," Uncle Harry said.

"Miz Martin has a new baby, Ma. Another boy." I knew she'd want to hear about that.

Uncle Harry related the rest of the story over supper.

"Poor Elizabeth," Ma fretted, "I wish I could go and help her, but Sarah's so delicate—and she hasn't had the measles."

"The Porters didn't have a cow, Josh," Matt murmured so only I could hear.

I ignored him.

Pa glanced at Sarah and nodded. "The blasted Indians stole their livestock—but at least they didn't burn them out."

The conversation about Indians went on and on. I only half listened. At my first opportunity, I slipped up the ladder to the loft and gathered some clothes together—then I located the journal and quill and pot of ink Ma had given me to improve my writing. "An unnecessary expense," Pa grumbled, when she gave them to me—but Ma had smiled and stood her ground. Ma put a lot of stock in learning and was proud of the fact that she had come from what she called "a gentle background." Ma grew up in Williamsburg. Unlike most women on the frontier, she could read and write. She'd taught Matt and me to read and write, as well.

Opening the journal, I took Lettie's rose out of my pouch and pressed it between the pages. Then I gathered everything into a bundle and hid it behind the wooden trunk Ma used to store extra bedding.

A little while later, Matt dropped onto the pallet beside me. "You awake?"

"I am now." I squelched the urge to pick a fight and try and make him tell me the truth about Bessy's disappearance.

"Don't you want to know what Pa was going to trade for the cow?"

When I didn't answer, he flopped on his belly and changed the subject. "How's Lettie?"

"What do you want to know for? I thought you didn't like her."

"I don't. She's just a squirt of a girl."

Not any more, she wasn't. Intriguing images of the new Lettie bloomed in my imagination. "She doesn't like you, either." Grinning, I turned on my side—away from him. I needed to work out my plan.

CHAPTER FOUR

ESCAPE

I woke up, my stomach fluttering. It was still dark—by my reckoning, around five o'clock. I rose from the pallet, careful not to make any noise that might rouse Matt or Uncle Harry, who had slept in the loft. Dressing quickly, I reached my hand behind Ma's trunk for my bundle. Uncle Harry turned over and muttered. I froze, the blood pounding in my ears, but he began to snore again.

I made my way down the ladder as a log from last night's fire shifted, releasing a shower of sparks. I glanced at the open doorway to the bedroom Ma and Pa shared with Sarah. All was quiet.

I lifted the door latch, pushed the rawhide door loop through the hole to the outside and inched the door open—then slipped through, carefully pulled the door closed, and pushed the loop back inside. It had sprinkled during the night. The air was cool. A loon cried out near the pond, and I heard something rustling in the bushes. I ran for the cover of the woods, the sound of my footsteps muted by my moccasins.

Pausing to catch my breath, I looked back at the cabin. It was dark inside. No one had wakened to light a candle. I padded to a forested area across from the barn and climbed the oak I had ripped my breeches on. The tree was enormous. They wouldn't be able to see me through the leaves.

It seemed an eternity before rays of sun spiked through the woods and laurel slicks surrounding the valley where our farm lay. At last, someone threw back the shutters.

From my hiding place, I watched Pa and Matt come out of the cabin and walk down the path to the barn. They seemed so at ease with each other. A sick feeling gathered in the pit of my stomach. Pa and his precious Matt. Pa had called me a liar. I had to lie to stay out of trouble! So what, I stretched the truth and was careless sometimes. None of that even compared to what Matt had done to me. It was Pa's and Matt's fault—me leaving home.

They brought Uncle Harry's team out of the barn and began to harness them.

"Where's Josh?" Uncle Harry was on the path, approaching the barn.

"Don't know," Matt answered. "Maybe he went hunting for squirrel."

Pa snorted. "When there's work to be done, you can count on Josh to find a way to wiggle out of it."

I shrank against the tree trunk, more certain than ever that my decision to run away was the right one.

Uncle Harry and Pa and Matt rolled the hogshead containing the tobacco out of the shed, grunting over the weight of it. With growing impatience, I watched the three of them rig a hoist. Pa and Matt pulled on the rope, and the hogshead swung into the air—then Uncle Harry pulled it into the wagon and set it in position. Releasing the rope, he tossed it back to Pa.

Pa coiled the rope and handed it to Matt. "Here, son—use this to tie down the hogshead and come on to breakfast." He headed for the cabin with Uncle Harry.

Matt began to loop the rope around the hogshead. Good old Matt—so reliable. He stopped what he was doing and looked in my direction! Had he seen me? No. He turned back to the hogshead and completed his task. Testing the rope with a final yank, he leaped to the ground and hurried to the cabin.

I climbed down the tree and threw my bundle into the wagon—
then pulled myself inside and looked around for someplace to hide.
Luck was with me. A large tarpaulin lay in the corner. I edged
myself down behind the hogshead, tugged on the rough canvas,
and pulled it over me.

Breathing deeply, I tried to calm myself by thinking about Fort
Cumberland. Uncle Harry said there would be two thousand men
there. In my mind's eye I could see them: militiamen from the
colonies and redcoats filled with a sense of patriotism and eager to
fight. They'd all have guns. The longrifle in the hay came to mind.
If only things had turned out differently.

I wished I could have told Lettie my plan—but yesterday, when
Uncle Harry and I were at Martin Plantation, I didn't know I was
going to run away. I tried not to think about Ma.

Voices! Holding the tarp close, I silenced my breathing and
held still.

The wagon jostled as Uncle Harry swung aboard. "Sorry to
miss Josh. Tell him I said goodbye." The brake squeaked when he
released it, and the team stepped forward.

"Whoa, Harry." My breath caught at the sound of Pa's voice
calling after us. "Let me check that hogshead one more time. If it
breaks loose, it'll play hell with your fancy wagon."

He climbed into the wagon bed, his feet just inches away from
me as he checked the rope securing the tobacco. I lay rigid under
the tarp, hardly daring to breathe, my heart thumping so hard I was
sure Pa could hear.

"It's all right," he said at last. "Matt did a good job on it." The
wagon rocked as he jumped to the ground.

Between the heat and not sleeping much last night, I was beginning to feel drowsy. It would take three hours, at least, to get to the
fort. I wiggled around, trying to get comfortable, and fell asleep.

The quiet when the wagon halted wakened me. Sweaty and
thirsty, I shoved the tarp aside and put my eye to a crack in the
wooden siding. We were on the top of a hill. Fort Cumberland lay
in a clearing below. The body of the fort backed up to a high v-

shaped bluff, with a creek along one side and a river on the other. I could see men in uniform setting up tents in front of the log wall surrounding it.

"What's going on?" Uncle Harry called to someone out of view. "The 48th Regiment just marched in," a voice floated back. "They're making camp down yonder."

I braced myself against the hogshead as Uncle Harry set the team in motion. The wagon wheeled down into the valley, squeaking when he applied the brake to keep it from running up on the horses.

When we came to a halt, the team shook themselves and blew. Uncle Harry climbed out of the wagon. I lifted the tarp in time to see him head toward the fort. He had promised Lettie's grandfather he would take the message about the plantation being burned to Mister—er—Captain Martin. That must be where he was headed.

I wriggled free of the canvas and tossed my bundle into the weeds. Jumping to the ground, I snatched it up and followed Uncle Harry, careful not to stay too close. I had already decided, if anyone stopped me and asked me why I was there, I'd tell them I was looking for my uncle—that he was needed at home.

Suddenly Uncle Harry turned toward me to answer someone's greeting! I darted behind a tent and held my breath. Seconds passed, and nothing happened. I peeked out and saw him enter a tent with a flag hanging on a pole beside it.

"Sir?" I called out to a man in buckskin passing by.

"You talkin' to me?"

"Yes, sir. Do you know whose tent that is?" I pointed.

"Why, the cap'n of the Virginia Militia, son."

I crept closer and heard a deep voice inside the tent say, "Yes, Corporal Bedford, what can I do for you?"

"I'm looking for Abram Martin, sir. I have a message for him."

"His brother-in-law was here last evening," the voice answered. "Martin resigned his commission and left before dawn this morning."

"That's all I need to know. Thank you, sir. I'll bid you good day."

40

Mister Martin was probably home by now. I slipped behind the tent and waited. When Uncle Harry walked back toward the Conestoga, I set out in the opposite direction trying my best to calm my nerves.

The camp was crowded with redcoats and militiamen. Caught up in the confusion, I began to feel hemmed in. I caught a glimpse of something blue. A skirt! What was a woman doing here? There were other women around the tents, most of them wearing drab gowns and petticoats. They all wore aprons. Puffy things Ma called mob caps covered their hair. Wives, I decided, after I heard one or two call out to men who were apparently their husbands. I came to the creek and gulped down handfuls of water. Downstream, women were on their knees doing their washing, surrounded by heaps of rumpled clothes.

The gates to the fort were open. Inside, I could see a large field. That must be the parade ground. I counted seven buildings, two of them flanking the gates. A pair of long buildings lay end to end on either side beyond them, and there was a rectangular building across the back.

I spied a woman coming out of one of the buildings. Her hair was neat under her mob cap and her gown and apron looked clean. She walked like a person with authority. Could she be a nurse? Was the building she came out of a hospital? Afraid of staying too long in one place, I hurried on.

A second train of wagons lay beyond the encampment where Uncle Harry had left his wagon. Separate camps? Horses were wandering loose, feeding on leaves and tree shoots. A plump woman with stringy black hair stood in the doorway of a tent. She caught my glance and grinned. Lifting her skirts, she showed her leg and beckoned to me. "Hey there, dearie—you with the blonde curls..."

I turned and ran. Something about her made my skin crawl.

The smell of food cooking over open fires reminded me that I hadn't eaten. I glanced at the sun. It was noon. Ma would be serving dinner—but maybe not today. The family would know by now that I hadn't gone hunting. As soon as Pa discovered I had taken extra

41

clothes, he'd guess I'd run away—and probably where. I tried not to think about Ma.

My stomach growled. When I hid in Uncle Harry's wagon, I never really thought about what I was going to eat or where I would sleep once I got to the fort. An empty feeling besides hunger crept into my stomach. Everybody seemed to fit in somehow. Everybody but me.

I came upon a woman stirring a pot over a campfire. She raised her head and smiled. I was tempted to ask her for something to eat. Then I remembered the woman who had called out to me earlier. I hurried away.

By mid-afternoon I was famished. I sat down under a tree on the outskirts of the fort and tried to figure out what to do. How could I have been so dumb as to think I'd find a place to stay and food to eat at the fort on my own? Most of the people I'd seen looked like they didn't have much. Some of the men didn't have any shoes! I could milk and tend chickens like I did at home and earn my way, but the only livestock I'd seen belonged to the militia. There'd be men assigned to handle their care. I could hoe a field or weed a garden—but there weren't any.

I stood up and brushed myself off. There wasn't any choice. I'd have to find Uncle Harry and turn myself in. I could already feel Pa's willow switch and see Matt's grinning face when Uncle Harry brought me home.

On my way to the Virginia Militia's camp, I saw two men in buckskin sitting beside a fire. One of the men was turning a couple of rabbits on a spit. He eyed me. "Lookin' fer somebody?"

The smell of the roasting meat made my mouth water. "No sir." My stomach growled. Embarrassed, I stared at the rabbits and made myself ask, "Uh… is there any work I can do?"

The men exchanged glances, and the man cooking grinned. "Rabbit's about done. Come set a while and eat while I think on it."

A seed of hope planted itself. I sat on the ground between the two men. The cook looked to be around twenty. Medium height and sturdy, he had wide cheekbones and hollow cheeks. The other man was small and wiry like Pa.

"What's your name?" the shorter man asked.

I couldn't use my own name, for fear it might somehow reach Uncle Harry. "J-Jed," I stammered, "Jed Beddington." I used the first name that came to mind.

"Glad to meet you, Jed. I'm John. John Finley. This here's Boone." He motioned to the cook. "You can call him Dan'l. Leastways that's what I call him, when he behaves. I have some other names fer him when he don't."

Daniel picked up a pebble and hit John with it. Clearly, the men were close friends.

"Where you from?" John asked.

"Uh..." I searched my mind for a believable answer. "Near Winchester," I lied. It was the nearest town, sixty miles southeast of Fort Cumberland.

Daniel looked at me. "You with kin?"

"Don't have any." My face burned at the lie.

"We're with the North Carolina Militia, Major Dobbs' command." Daniel pointed to John and teased, "If I'd knowed he was gonna be here, I wouldn't of come."

There were different camps. I relaxed a little. A Virginian, Uncle Harry probably wouldn't have much to do with the men from North Carolina. Less chance he'd find out I was there.

John guffawed. "Don't give me that, Dan'l. Wild horses couldn't of kept you from comin'. I know you've got a little gal tucked away in Pennsylvania."

Daniel's face turned red. "Haven't seen her since I moved to Carolina, nigh on to five years ago. She's probably married now, with kids."

He sliced off a rabbit leg with a stroke of his knife. "Here, try some of this." He handed it to me.

I bit into the tasty meat, swiped at the dribbling juice with the back of my hand, and wiped it on my breeches—glad Ma wasn't there to correct me.

"We're wagoners," Daniel said. "Reckon I could use some help.

43

How handy are you with a team?"

"I—uh—I know about horses," I said, my mouth full of rabbit. I couldn't tell Daniel that Pa wouldn't let me drive our team. "I've driven a Conestoga," I boasted.

Daniel and John exchanged glances again.

"If you'll tell me what you want me to do, I'm sure I can do it," I said.

Daniel looked at John. "He reminds me of my little brother I was tellin' you about." He gave me a long look. "Need a place to stay?"

I nodded.

"You can bunk in the wagon."

A job and a place to stay! Wouldn't that just about kill Matt? I grinned at the thought.

We finished the rabbit. Daniel showed me around his campsite—stopping now and then to say something to John. Suddenly, my ears picked up an unfamiliar sound. "What's that?" I asked.

"The 48th Regiment," John said, standing up . "We been expectin' 'em."

The piping fifes and beating drums grew louder as we pushed our way through the crowd toward the parade ground.

"That there's the Potomac." Daniel pointed to the river. "The water on the other side of the fort, where the women are doin' their washin', is Wills Creek."

BOOM! BOOM! BOOM! One by one, the guns of Fort Cumberland roared. I pressed forward, eager to see.

A soldier marched into view carrying a pole—the red, white, and blue flag of the British Empire waving on the end of it. Behind him came the drummers and fifers, setting the pace for the men marching behind them. I struggled to remember the date. It was the 10th… the 10th of May… 1755. I vowed that I would never forget it.

"That there's the general." Daniel pointed to a man in a red uniform trimmed with shiny gold braid. Mounted on a fine black gelding, General Braddock was leading some other officers on horseback onto the parade ground.

The general was old and fat! Disappointed, I turned my attention to a tall man riding behind him. "Who's that—the one on the bay?"

"Colonel—er—Cap'n Washington," Daniel corrected himself. Pa didn't like Captain Washington. Curious, I looked him over. He was wearing a red and white uniform with a blue cloak, his dark brown hair pulled back in a queue under a black tricorne. "How old is he?" I asked.

"Twenty-three," Daniel said. "Three years older'n me." Officers waiting at the end of the field snapped to attention and saluted. General Braddock signaled for the reading of his orders, which included Captain Washington's appointment as his colonial aide de camp. Then the general dismounted and disappeared inside the building at the end of the parade ground.

The British regulars who had marched in behind General Braddock and his officers broke ranks and began to walk away. One of them passed by me. He wore a red coat and vest trimmed with white braid and red breeches. His hat was black. So was the pouch hanging from his white leather belt. He was armed with a musket and bayonet. The musket looked lighter and handier than the longrifles I was used to. I eyed it, wishing I could hold it.

"Let's go, Jed," Daniel said. "Jed?"

Forgetting my new name, I didn't answer. By the time I turned around, he had cut through the crowd with John and disappeared.

In my hurry to catch up, I ran into a fat boy in uniform walking with some others, and we both went sprawling. I scrambled to my feet and held out a hand to help him up.

The redcoat pushed it away and struggled to stand. "Why don't ye watch where you're goin'," he sneered, with a thick Irish accent. Looking at his friends, he added, "Or ain't you colonists smart 'nough to do that?"

I balled my fists and was ready to fight, when a tall thin boy in red uniform wedged himself between us. "T'was an accident, boyo."

He looked older than me. Ugly, I thought at first. He had a beaky nose splotched with freckles, red hair, hazel eyes, and ears that stuck out from his head like handles. Then he smiled, and I knew at once we could be friends. There was no time for that now. Afraid of the attention I had attracted, I broke through the ring of people crowding around us and high-tailed it back to Daniel's wagon.

CHAPTER FIVE

SETTLING IN

I poked my head out of the wagon, sniffed the morning air, and looked beyond the tree-covered mountains at the sky. It was almost dawn. Few people were stirring. There was no sign of Daniel. Pulling out my sling, I tested the strength of its leather thong, stuck it in my belt, and jumped to the ground.

I headed for the woods, set on surprising Daniel by bringing in some game for our noonday meal. The area was strange to me, making me edgy.

A squirrel chattered overhead, perched on the branch of a maple tree. I pulled a pebble from my pouch, armed my sling and let fly. The squirrel fell to the ground. I was reaching down to pick it up when the birds in the forest hushed. The hair rose on the back of my neck. I forgot about the squirrel and hid in the thicket.

Silent as ghosts, eight dark-skinned men filed past me. I thought of the longrifle I had discovered in the barn and wished for it desperately.

The first Indian had a tomahawk tattooed on his chest and bows and arrows tattooed on his cheeks. The younger brave that followed resembled him. All the men wore war paint. Their ears had been cut from the upper rims to their earlobes, and their heads were shaved except for a lock of hair hanging down with feathers tied to it. They were armed with tomahawks and longrifles.

When the last of them disappeared, I breathed a sigh of relief—just as a hard something pressed into the small of my back. I spun around. The lead Indian had poked me with his gun. The other savages surrounded me. I was trapped!

The younger warrior grabbed my sling. The Indians gabbled among themselves and he handed it back, motioning to me to show him how to use it. I groped in my pouch for a rock, my fingers trembling so much that I dropped it. The other Indians giggled. He pointed to a tree knot. I scooped up the rock, placed it in my sling—then swung and released it, hitting the target. The savages mimicked me, laughing—until the lead Indian grunted and led them away.

The bushes parted and Daniel bounded to my side.

"Why didn't you shoot 'em?" I cried, shaken.

"And have the whole goldarn army on my tail?"

"What do you mean?"

"That was Monacathothe—Half King—with his son and some of his braves. They're allies. I heard he'd be comin' into the fort today. They're goin' to have a congress with Braddock."

"A what?"

"A meetin'. What're you doin' here?"

"I was hunting," I said, angry that Daniel had seen how scared I was.

"With that?" He pointed at my sling.

If there was one thing I prided myself on, it was my sling. "Yes—sir," I said, scowling. I located the dead squirrel and picked it up.

Something flickered in Daniel's eyes and vanished. Was he laughing at me?

"C'mon," he said. "A longrifle's easier."

Trailing along behind him, I said, "If those Indians are friendly, why are they wearing war paint?"

"It's good camouflage in the forest and makes 'em look fierce—and it's their Sunday best, in case they get killed. They want to look good when they meet the Great Spirit."

Daniel turned to face me, a finger to his lips. There, half-hidden by a branch some twenty yards away, a huge bear sat on his haunches scooping termites out of a log.

I stepped forward to get a better look and a twig under my foot snapped. Dang! The bear lumbered to his feet and lifted his nose, sniffing the air for scent. Daniel motioned to me to back off

Focused on the bear, I tripped over a root and grabbed a branch to keep from falling. The branch was dry. It broke, making a cracking noise. The bear charged.

"Tarnation, Jed, you went and did it!" Leveling his rifle, Daniel took aim and fired. The bear thudded to the ground, a gory hole where his eye had been.

I could feel the blood pumping through my body. "Sorry," I mumbled, mortified that I had been so careless. If it hadn't been for Daniel... in my mind's eye, I could see Matt pointing at me and laughing.

"No harm done—this time." Daniel blew down the gun barrel to clear it, reached for the powder horn attached to his belt, and poured powder into the longrifle's muzzle—then rammed home a ball and primed the pan, preparing the gun to fire again. He leaned it against the trunk of an oak tree.

We hung the bear from a limb by his hind legs, struggling because of his weight. Daniel cut his throat to drain the blood—then I held him while he skinned him. I helped him lower the carcass. We hung the bear again, head up, and Daniel sliced his belly and cleaned out his guts.

All this time, he hadn't said a word. The silence was uncomfortable. "Don't you wish you had a musket like the redcoats'?" I asked.

"What fer? Shootin' doesn't get any better'n this."

"I think I'd want one of theirs."

He hunkered down, warming to the subject. "You ever use a gun—you bein' a orphan and all..."

"Lots of times." Daniel would know that. It was a given on the frontier that women and children big enough to handle a gun would know how to shoot.

Daniel hoisted his eleven-pound gun like it was a feather. "I know this here rifle like I know the freckles on the back of my hand. There's no British musket in the world that can beat it. Did you know the redcoats use cartridges in their muskets? Cartridges!" He spat the word.

"Seems to me they'd save a lot of time."

"But think of the waste. I know just how much powder to use fer every target." His mind was set, reminding me of Pa. I didn't want to argue with him. "How is it you know so much about the woods?" I changed the subject.

Daniel snorted. "Had my own place since I was younger'n you. Built it myself."

"How come?"

"With six brothers, I needed the peace and quiet."

I was boggled by the thought of seven boys living under the same roof, when I couldn't stand even one. "What're we going to do with all this meat?" I said, looking at the bear.

"We'll take some to Cap'n Washington." Daniel slid the flat of his bloody knife blade against the grass to clean it. "By the way, Jed, a man and his son came by the wagon after you left this mornin'. They were lookin' fer a lad named Josh Bedford. Said he was a runaway."

Pa and Matt! Our eyes met. I looked at his mouth, afraid of his next words. But he busied himself with his knife.

"Well, that does it," he said at last. He stuck the knife in his scabbard. "C'mon. We'll take some of this back to camp and come back fer the rest."

We wrapped a hunk of the bear meat in the bearskin, careful that the fur didn't touch it and taint the taste. I kept looking at Daniel as I helped him lug it back to his tent. Would he turn me in? What should I do? If Pa learned for sure that I was at the fort, he would hound me until he brought me to ground.

Back at our camp, Daniel hacked off some of the meat and covered it with a piece of deer hide. "C'mon, Jed, I'll introduce you to the cap'n."

There was nothing to do but go with him. I walked beside him through the encampment, ready to bolt as I glanced about looking for Pa and Matt and Uncle Harry. When we reached Captain Washington's tent, he was putting on his tricorne to go somewhere.

"Daniel... Daniel Boone," he said, "What can I do for you?"

"Sir. Thought you might like to have some bear meat fer your dinner. This here's Jed—Jed Beddington, from Winchester." Daniel motioned to me.

He didn't know I was the runaway! I began to relax.

"Jed." Washington nodded. "I'm on my way to General Braddock's quarters to meet with Half King and his braves. Leave the meat with John Alton, my orderly—and thank you, Daniel."

I studied the captain. He was taller even than Uncle Harry. He had a long nose and a thin face that made his eyes look too close together. His eyes were icy blue.

Washington's orderly came into the tent as the captain left. Daniel handed him the packet of bear meat. While they visited, I passed the time looking around. There was a narrow camp bed, a folding chair, and a table with writing implements on it. A book lay open in the middle of the table, beside a half-spent candle. I glanced at the open pages. It was a journal.

"Let's go, Jed." Daniel beckoned to me.

I caught a glimpse of two people walking by as he thrust his broad shoulders through the entrance to the tent. Pa and Matt! I shrank away, out of sight.

Daniel wheeled and gave me a sharp look—then stepped outside, blocking the opening. "Any luck findin' your boy, Mister Bedford?"

"Not yet," Pa answered. "Keep an eye out for him, will you? If you run across him, take him to his uncle, Harry Bedford, with the Virginia Militia. He'll see to it that Josh gets home." To Matt he said, "Let's get going, son. Your ma will be needing us."

Daniel backed into the tent. He turned around and looked at me. It was over. There was no question about him knowing who I was now. I glanced at Mister Alton. He was outside the tent, preparing the bear meat for the spit. Absorbed in his task, he seemed unaware of what had happened. "You know, don't you?" I said.

"I suspected."

"Why didn't you tell them?"

"Figured you must have your reasons fer leavin' home." He poked his head outside the tent and looked around. "They're gone. C'mon. We'll talk about it later."

We drove the wagon as far into the forest as we could and loaded the rest of the bear meat. When we got back to camp, Daniel set some of it over the open spit to roast and began cutting the rest into strips to dry for jerky. "So, why did you come to Fort Cumberland, Jed—or is it Josh?"

"Jed." I'd been sitting beside the campfire, watching him carve the meat. "I don't want Uncle Harry to hear my name and find out I'm here." I picked up a twig and tossed it into the flames.

He nodded.

"I mostly ran away because Pa hates me—and my brother and I don't get along."

"Why does your pa hate you?"

I never had to put it into words before. I took a minute to think. "No matter what I do, I can't please him," I said at last. "Pa's mad at me all the time."

"Any of it your fault?"

I squirmed, uncomfortable with the way the conversation was going. "Ma thinks I'm not reliable."

He could have pinned me to the wall, right then and there by asking why. Instead, he stopped slicing the meat and looked at me. "Tell me about your brother."

"We fight all the time."

"I don't get along with my brothers sometimes," Daniel said. "First one and then another of 'em ''ll get under my skin." He started working on the meat again.

"This is different, Dan'l. Matt betrayed me." I told him about Matt's sling, how it broke, and about the fight afterwards. Then I came to the part about Bessy. "Pa was sure the cow got out because I was careless. He blam— "

Daniel interrupted me. "And you? Did you think it was your fault?"

I looked at the fire and slowly nodded. "But Matt let me take the blame." Helping Daniel hang the strips of bear meat to dry, I told him the rest of the story.

In late afternoon, Daniel sent me to fetch water from Wills Creek. I was filling the pail when I heard a fife upstream. Dumping out the water, I went to investigate.

The boy who broke up my fight with the redcoat was sitting on a rock, his bare feet soaking in the creek. Caught up in his music, he was startled when I said, "What's that you're playing?"

"Greensleeves. Ain't it grand?" He put the fife to his lips and piped it again. "Are y'alright?" he asked when he finished.

I wasn't sure what he meant. I held out the empty pail.

"Me name's Oliver, boyo—Oliver Cunningham, from Cork. I'm with the 48th Regiment." He held out his hand.

Shaking it, I answered, "Beddington—Jed Beddington, from Winchester." The lie came easier now.

"Have ye been in any donnybrooks of late?" Oliver grinned.

"I could've whipped your friend."

"No friend of mine—and I was only funnin'." He looked me over. "How auld're ye?"

How old was he? "F-fifteen," I answered, hoping my height would carry the lie.

"Me, too," he said, clearly pleased we were the same age. His smile faded. "Watch out for that Willie. He's a sly one."

CHAPTER SIX

TRIALS

I woke to the sound of drums calling the redcoats to get up and get moving. During the few days I had been at Fort Cumberland, I had come to recognize the different beats telling them what to do. I yawned. Looking through the tailgate of the wagon, I listened to the chirps of waking birds and admired the rosy streaks stretching across the sky.

I jumped to the ground. Daniel had already set a fire. A pot of something hung over the flames. I lifted the lid. Porridge. I brought a wooden trencher from the wagon and helped myself—then made for Wills Creek and washed up before heading back to do chores.

Daniel had gone someplace. Unlike Pa, he pretty much let me figure out what I was supposed to do and when I was supposed to do it.

It was still early when I started to groom Daniel's gelding. The horse swished his tail, trying to dislodge a deer fly on his flank. "Pesky fly—leave Buck alone!" I swatted at it with my currycomb.

Brushing Buck's sleek coat, I thought about how my life had changed. I could hardly believe I was at Fort Cumberland. I had a job... a place to stay, friends.... I had sneaked into the Virginia Militia's camp a few times for a glimpse of Uncle Harry. He was always the center of attention, joking and telling stories—his face flushed with what I guessed was more than his daily half-cup ration of rum. The last time I saw him he was gambling. It was a side of Uncle Harry I hadn't expected.

The last few evenings, Oliver had dropped by and visited. We'd sat around the campfire, discussing things with Daniel and John. I loved it that they treated us like men. Pa and I never discussed anything.

Last night, Daniel had made jerky stew and said I could invite Oliver to eat with us. John was there, of course. Over our meal, I told them about the Gregorsons. "Why are the Indians so blasted mean?" I asked when I finished my story.

"We have a history of doin' 'em out of land that's been theirs ferever," Daniel said.

"And do the French rob 'em of their land as well?" Oliver asked.

Daniel nodded. "They have better ways of doin' it, though." He set his trencher aside and took out his pipe.

"What do you mean?" I said.

Daniel had filled his pipe with tobacco and lit it with a stick from the campfire. Exhaling a stream of smoke, he said, "They learn their language. Some of 'em even marry squaws."

"They're mostly interested in tradin' fer furs, which suits them Injuns just fine," John said.

"That must be why some tribes've joined the French," Oliver said.

"Most of 'em," John muttered, his face grim.

"What about us?" I asked.

"Our folks're settlers," Daniel said. "We mostly farm and build towns."

John tossed a stick into the fire. "The savages don't like us, 'cause we're drivin' the game away from their huntin' grounds."

"Then why would any of 'em be willin' to fight for the Crown?" Oliver asked. "We sell 'em better guns and cheaper blankets, and keep 'em in English rum," Daniel answered.

"Don't forget the redskins who won't join either side," John had said. "They hate us. Truth is—given half a chance, most of them Injuns'ud gladly scalp us."

I thought about Half King and the fifty or so Indians with families living at Fort Cumberland. They kept to themselves most of the time, but just knowing they were camped nearby made me uneasy.

"Boyo!"

The sound of Oliver's voice yanked me back to the present. He ran toward me waving his hand.

"There's been a court-martial," he gasped. "They handed down sentences. The men're to be punished right now!"

I tossed the currycomb in the wagon and raced him to the parade ground. A blindfolded man stood tied to a post. A crowd of people had gathered to watch.

"Who's that?" I pointed to an officer who appeared to be in charge.

"That be Colonel Gage. He presided over the court-martial."

Six British soldiers in full uniform marched onto the field and took their places. The bystanders murmured and fell silent as one of them stepped forward.

"What're they going to do, Oliver?" I whispered, looking at the redcoats.

"That there's the sergeant. He'll be issuin' orders to shoot the man."

"What?"

"He's a deserter, boyo. He's been sentenced to die."

"Ready..." the sergeant barked. The redcoats picked up their muskets and leveled them.

"Aim..." the sergeant barked. The firing squad aimed their guns at the prisoner.

I closed my eyes.

"FIRE!"

The air rang with gunshots. I opened my eyes and saw the prisoner's body hanging, limp and bleeding, against the post. "Let's go." I yanked at Oliver's sleeve.

"Wait, lad! There's more."

Three shirtless prisoners were marched forward and lined up.

A pair of redcoats untied the rope binding one of the men's wrists and tied his upraised arms to a post while another soldier stepped forward holding a whip.

"One..." the sergeant barked.

I flinched as the whip whined and a bloody wound appeared on the man's bare back.

"Two..." the sergeant barked.

Over and over the whip snaked through the air, biting into the man's back and snatching away bits of skin. "For gosh sake, Oliver, let's get out of here!" I pleaded, when the convict received his hundredth stripe. I couldn't bear to watch another minute, and there were two more prisoners to go.

"What in the world did those men do to be flogged that way?" I asked, as we left the awful scene.

"They were chancers—got to drinkin' and stole a keg of beer from a sutler."

"What's that?"

"One of the peddlers who's been skinnin' 'em with over-priced goods."

It didn't seem fair for them to be punished that way. I thought of Uncle Harry, carousing with his friends, and hoped he wouldn't do anything to get himself in trouble.

Oliver had to get back to his regiment. When I reached the wagon, Daniel was waiting for me.

"Where's my lead horse, Jed? Where's Buck?"

I recognized the look on Daniel's face: the set lips and the anger. It could have been Pa standing there. I glanced around for the missing gelding with a feeling of panic. What had I done? I'd tossed the currycomb into the wagon. Oliver was in a hurry. Oh my gosh, I had forgotten to tether Buck before I left!

"I'll give you one hour to find him." Daniel sounded exactly like Pa.

I turned and ran, my throat aching. Where should I look? I combed the area around our immediate camp. No luck. I went to the place on the outskirts of Fort Cumberland where I had first seen horses grazing. Buck wasn't there, either. Wait! My heart skipped a beat. I ran toward a horse half-hidden by some bushes—but it wasn't Buck.

I searched the wooded area skirting the fort—through stands of maples and oaks and pine trees, retracing my steps over and over again, calling for Buck, cussing him for taking off and hating myself for being so careless.

I looked at the sun. A lot more than an hour had passed. Daniel wasn't the kind of man to go back on his word. I wanted to scream. I'd never make it at Fort Cumberland—any more than I had at home! Ma was right. I wasn't reliable. Daniel would never forgive me. I was certain of it.

I headed for Wills Creek and slumped down on a rock. First there was the bear, now this. I could go to Uncle Harry, but then what? He'd take me home. I could just see it—Pa whipping me, and Matt standing in the corner looking smug. I stared at the flowing water, wishing the earth would just open up and swallow me, like in the Bible. At least then, I wouldn't have to think anymore

"Jed?"

"Hello, Oliver." I looked at the water again.

"Dan'l's been askin' for ye."

"What did he want?" I dreaded his answer.

"Somebody discovered his horse and brung him back. Dan'l wanted ye to know. He had somethin' else on his mind, too."

I stood up, my knees shaking. "When? How? Where did they find him?"

"Don't know," he said breezily.

Daniel hadn't told him about Buck.

"The 44th is comin' in—some of it. Let's go watch."

I could hear the drums in the distance. "I have to talk to Dan'l first."

We made their way back to camp, but Daniel wasn't there. I hurried over to Buck, tethered to the wagon, and threw my arms around his neck.

"Hurry, Jed—or we're goin' to miss it."

We arrived at the parade ground just as the regiment marched in. Looking at the redcoats' splendid uniforms and listening to the drums, I couldn't understand why Daniel wasn't impressed by General Braddock's troops.

Oliver and I had discussed with Daniel and John the advantages of the redcoats' disciplined way of shooting volleys on command compared with the way we fought in the colonies: hugging the ground, hiding behind bushes, and dodging from tree to tree as we picked out our targets.

"Ye know yerself, there're more of us and we're trained better," Oliver said.

"The redcoats'll mow the French down, Dan'l," I backed him up.

"Not in the woods, they won't."

"Just wait. You'll see," John had agreed with Daniel.

I was so busy watching the men of the 44th march in that I was shocked when someone dropped a hand on my shoulder and spun me around. Willie!

"Been thinkin' about ye, boyo," Willie snarled. "Nobody knocks me down and gets away with it—'specially not a colonist!'"

He socked me on the mouth, splitting my lip. It took me a few seconds to get my bearings. He struck again, but I was ready this time. I hit him back, trading blow for blow, using every trick I had learned in my tangles with Matt.

Willie charged and I jumped him, clinging as we both fell scuffling to the ground. Nose to nose, I could see his rotted teeth, the pimples scattered across his cheeks. He flung me off with a grunt. We circled each other. Blood ran down my chin and dripped onto my shirt as I dodged from side to side, out of reach. I feinted with my left hand and Willie dodged into my right fist. A cut opened over his right eye.

"Attaboy, Jed!" someone yelled.

Daniel! I wheeled to look and caught a blow to the jaw. Other voices called out, encouraging me—answered by redcoats rooting for Willie. Suddenly the fight between us spread as redcoats and colonials and camp women jumped into the fray, including Daniel. "Cease and desist!" General Braddock rode through the crowd on his black horse.

The mob broke up. Some of Willie's friends gathered around him. They gave me some ugly looks, and I knew they were talking about me. Suddenly, I missed Oliver. I hadn't seen him since the fight started.

I turned away and saw Daniel. He waved, and I hurried toward him, eager to make sure he wasn't still angry with me over the horse.

There was a red lump on his right cheek and one of his eyes was nearly swollen shut. "You're a sight fer sore eyes, Jed," he said, grinning.

"You don't look so good, yourself." I licked my sore lip, trying to think of the right thing to say. Apologizing had always been hard for me. "About Buck—"

"You're lucky he was found." He gave me a hard look—then, unlike Pa, dropped the painful subject. "I was lookin' fer you, when that redcoat picked the fight."

"How come?"

"The general's tired of waitin' fer Cap'n Cresap to show up with the flour he ordered. He's sendin' thirty wagons to Winchester fer provisions, includin' mine. John's goin', too."

"Is that the same man who sold the army the bad beef?"

He shook his head. "His son—a scoundrel, just like his pa. Seems to run in the family. C'mon, we have to get ready."

"How long will we be gone?"

"Long as it takes."

I held back. "Oliver and I were together, when Willie picked the fight. I don't know what happened to him."

Daniel shrugged. "Maybe he sided with the redcoats."

Would Oliver do that? He was my friend! "I can't go with you," I said. "I need to talk to Oliver."

"What'll you do?"

"I'll figure out something."

"Suit yourself."

I stared at him. Daniel didn't care whether I went with him or not! Maybe he was holding a grudge, after all. I didn't know what to do. I wanted to fix things with Daniel, but the bad feeling I had about Oliver wouldn't go away. I walked with Daniel back to the wagon and helped him harness the team. Then I gathered up my things.

"Here, Jed, better have some of this." Daniel tossed me some biscuit and a hunk of dried beef.

"Thanks." I dropped my bundle on the ground and jumped down next to it. "See you when you get back."

CHAPTER SEVEN

REPRIEVE

Watching Daniel pull out to join the other wagons going to Winchester, I started to worry. What was I going to do? Had I made the right decision? I thought about Oliver and went to find him.

I climbed the hill to the 48th Regiment's camp. The redcoats eyed me as I moved among their tents, their faces sullen and angry. When I came to the area where the drummers and fifers were quartered, I found Willie seated beside a campfire, along with some others.

"Damn you!" He tried to lunge at me, but the other boys grabbed him and held him back.

Willie's hurt eye was swollen shut. "I'm looking for Oliver Cunningham," I said.

"Look someplace else," someone snapped.

"Maybe I'll just do that." I sauntered away, taking my time. Soon as I was out of sight, I ran down the hill, through the woods, to the creek. Sure enough, Oliver was on our rock, his red hair shining in the sunlight.

He heard me and stood up. Our eyes met. He didn't say anything.

There was a problem! The fight... what had he done? Had he turned against me?

"I been thinkin', boyo."

I held my breath. What was he going to say?

"Willie shouldna' ha' picked that fight. You runnin' into him was a wee accident." His Irish accent was so thick I had to really listen to understand his words. "I ha' to tell ye, boyo—when the lads from Cork got into the donnybrook, I didn't know what to do."

I nodded and swallowed.

"But we have the same king."

I nodded again.

"And the reason we came, in the first place, is to fight the French."

What was he getting at? I held my breath.

"What I'm tryin' to say is—there's no cause fer trouble between you and me, boyo. We're friends, ain't we?" He grinned and stuck out his hand.

I grabbed it. "We sure enough are."

We sat down on the rock.

"I told ye Willie was a sly one," he said.

"I'm going to get even with him. You'd better know that."

He tossed a pebble into the creek. "He's stepped on my toes a time or two. What're yer plans, then?"

"I'll let you know. By the way, Dan'l's gone to Winchester for supplies."

"And ye're not with him? I'd 've thought ye'd welcome a visit home."

I was tempted to tell Oliver that I wasn't from Winchester. But then I'd have to confess the other lies I had told him. I'd have to tell him about Matt and Pa, about how I'd run away, and that I wasn't fifteen or even fourteen. I couldn't risk it.

"There's... uh... no home to go to," I said.

"What do ye mean?"

I looked at the water. "I'm an orphan."

Oliver's face softened. "Ye mean—no family at all?"

I peeked through my lashes to see his reaction.

His freckled face drooped with sympathy. "Why didn't ye tell me?"

"I don't like to talk about it." That much was true. "C'mon, Oliver, let's catch us some fish."

I pulled a couple of lines with weighted hooks from my pouch, found some branches to tie them to, and baited them with some of Daniel's jerky. Oliver and I each took one. We sat down on our rock and tossed our lines into the water.

A dragonfly buzzed over the creek and hovered, its wings shining. I relaxed, watching it—the sun warm on my back. Why couldn't Matt and I talk about things the way Oliver and I did? Why couldn't we work things out, instead of always fighting? A mosquito hummed in my ear. I brushed it away. My thoughts turned to Fort Cumberland and some of the things that had happened. Turning to Oliver, I said, "Can I ask you a question?"

"What?"

"I was surprised to find women here."

"Why would that surprise ye? Far as I know, the only time lasses aren't allowed on a campaign is aboard a vessel. Sailors think they're bad luck."

"Uh... one woman acted sort of funny with me."

"How do ye mean, funny?"

"I never saw her before, but she called me over and... uh... sort of... wanted to talk to me."

Oliver put a hand to his hair, fluffed it, and batted his eyes. "Ye mean—like this?"

I laughed and nodded. "Sort of."

"You're fifteen, Jed. Don't ye know anythin' about lasses?"

"N-not much, I reckon." I concentrated on my fishing.

"The woman you saw was a harlot. She offers herself to men fer money."

"She sells her body? Why?"

"Think, Jed—what do animals do?"

"General Braddock allows that?"

Oliver smiled. "It's a given."

I pulled in a perch, threaded it through the mouth and gill with a viney branch, and jammed the stringer into the muddy creek bottom. Oliver watched me bait my hook and throw it back in the water.

"Is there a lass ye're sweet on?"

"Hadn't thought about it." It wasn't true. I had thought a lot about it. I checked the drying rose pressed between the pages of my journal every day. The journal was safely tucked inside my shirt that very minute. I ducked my head, so Oliver couldn't see my eyes and know I was lying, wishing I could tell him about Lettie. "How about you? You have a sweetheart?"

Oliver's face glowed. "Her name's Tibby—or I call her Tibby. Her real name's Tabitha Boggs. Her da's a sailor in His Majesty's fleet." He pulled out a miniature attached to a cord looped around his neck.

The face staring back at me didn't compare with Lettie's, even though the girl's picture had been poorly painted. "She's pretty," I tried to sound convincing.

"Not really—but she's a fine lass, and I love her anyway. I'm not so fair, meself." Oliver's lips parted in a happy smile. "We're promised. We'll be wed, soon as I get back to Ireland." He slipped the picture inside his shirt and stood up.

"Stay, and we'll cook the fish," I said.

"I'd like to, but I have duty this afternoon. Let me know what ye decide to do 'bout Willie." He grinned and disappeared in the brush.

Suddenly lonesome, I began to have second thoughts. Maybe I should have gone with Daniel after all—but if I had, I wouldn't have had the chance to talk to Oliver and make sure things were all right. I decided to go back to where Daniel and I had camped. The campfire would still be there. I could cook the perch and come up with a plan.

I pulled in the fishing line and stringer and was ready to leave, when I heard the whinny of a horse and a gruff voice coming from the other side of the thicket.

"Ye gods, with all the horses around did you have to go and steal that one?"

"But it's a good 'un."

"Too good. They'll be after us in no time."

I peered through the leaves and saw two men in buckskin leading a couple of geldings. Deserters! I drew a stone from inside my pouch, slipped my sling from under my belt, armed it, and let fly shouting, "Horse thieves!"

"Holy Jehoshaphat!" The smaller of the two men screamed and dropped the reins of the horse he was leading to grab at his neck. His companion leaped on the other horse, reached down for his partner's hand, and swung him up behind him. They crashed through the trees and vanished.

I plunged through the brush, recognizing at once the horse they had left behind. Captain Washington's bay! I picked up his reins, stroked the gelding's velvety muzzle, and led him back to the fort—trying to decide the best way to return him.

I tethered the horse to a sapling. Screwing up my courage, I approached the captain's tent. "If you please, sir, is Captain Washington here?" I asked Mister Alton, his orderly.

"No, he's not."

"I need to see him."

"Come in. You're welcome to wait. He's meeting with General Braddock and the other officers, but he should be back soon." Mister Alton rattled on, seemingly glad of the company.

Captain Washington ducked into the tent. "What's Ranger doing there, tied to a tree?"

I hesitated. Nervous, I stammered, "I f-found him in the w-woods, sir."

"A good horse goes," he said good-naturedly "—but it appears that Ranger got up and went." He smiled, clearly trying to set me at ease. In a stern voice he added, "Look into this, John. Someone has been remiss in his duty."

I forced myself to speak up. "Your horse didn't wander off, sir. Deserters stole him. I... uh... changed their plans." I patted the sling tucked under my belt.

"I see." He studied my face. "Aren't you the lad who came here with Boone the other day?"

I nodded.

"Where is Daniel?"

"Gone to Winchester, sir—for supplies."

"And you? I assumed that the two of you were together. What are you doing, now that he's gone?"

I shrugged.

"You have done me a service by returning my horse. Would you like to have the responsibility of caring for him—at least until Boone returns?"

"Yes, sir, I would," I said, grinning.

"It's settled, then. Mister Alton will arrange a place for you to stay."

All of a sudden, I thought about Buck. "Don't worry about Ranger, sir. I'll take good care of him."

I went back to Daniel's campsite for my bundle. When I returned, Mister Alton showed me around and gave me instructions. "You'll sleep in the wagon," he said.

How would you feel, Pa, if you could see me now? I couldn't help but wonder.

CHAPTER EIGHT

STRANGE CUSTOMS

The sun slipped behind the mountains and the drums began to beat retreat. The flag—which was raised every morning at first light, inched down the flagpole to be stowed for the night. I had been at the fort a little over a week.

I searched the crowd, looking for Oliver. Mister Alton was standing a few yards away. I waved to him—then turned to watch the ceremony unfolding on the parade ground.

General Braddock and his officers stood at attention to the right of the flagpole. I recognized Half King and some other Indians standing on the other side. Soldiers from the train of artillery were positioned in the middle of the field, beside three howitzers.

Mister Alton came up and stood beside me.

"Those cannons are huge," I said. "How did they get here?"

"It took thirty seamen to drag them here from the river with block and tackle."

"Prime!" a redcoat shouted.

The soldiers poured gunpowder into the cannons' firing pans.

"Charge!"

The shells were rammed down the barrels.

"FIRE!"

The redcoats touched the priming powder with punks. Belching smoke, the guns spewed their shells into the evening sky. Half King and the other Indians recoiled, clearly frightened.

"General Braddock staged this ceremony to impress them," Mister Alton said.

"How do you mean, sir?"

"Indians are scared to death of cannon. The general thought this would show Half King and his braves how we terrorize our enemies."

"My friend Oliver planned to meet me here, but I haven't seen him," I said.

"The drum majors have been instructed to march with their companies to the head of the artillery and await further orders, Jed. He's probably among them."

"Does that mean we'll be moving out? The supply wagons haven't come back from Winchester."

Mister Alton smiled. "Probably not."

When the ceremony was over, I told Mister Alton good night. He patted my shoulder and went on his way.

I followed the crowd leaving the parade ground. On the outskirts of the Indian encampment I could see squaws, bobbing and swaying to the beat of tom-toms, surrounded by a circle of men.

"What's going on?" I asked a ranger.

He chuckled. "An old Indian custom. Once or twice a year a squaw picks out a man she fancies and dances with him. She... uh..." he stopped what he was saying and looked at me. "She's... friendly with him for a week and then goes back to her husband."

I watched, fascinated, as woman after woman stopped dancing to take a soldier's hand and lead him into the woods. All of a sudden, one of the squaws looked at the ranger beside me — or so I thought. She was cockeyed, and it was hard to tell.

"That's Bright Lightning," the ranger said.

She was dressed in a buckskin skirt and tunic. When she grinned, I could see she had a mouthful of stained brown teeth. I turned away as she came close. The bear grease she had used to dress her hair smelled awful.

I glanced at the man beside me. Surely, he wouldn't go anywhere with such a woman. Then I realized it wasn't the ranger she was after. The crowd cheered as she grabbed my arm. I broke away and started to run. The men hooted and slapped each other on the back when Bright Lightning tackled me.

"Whoa there, missy," a deep voice rumbled.

Pinned by the squaw's stocky body, I struggled to look up. Uncle Harry! I wriggled out from under Bright Lightning and managed to stand.

"This no man," Uncle Harry said to her. "Him boy."

Bright Lightning grinned. "Pretty boy. Make man."

My face burned as the men around me snickered.

"No." Uncle Harry reached in his pouch and pulled out his flask. "This better. Drink firewater—no need man."

I held my breath as the squaw's eyes shifted from me to the liquor. She snatched the flask and danced away.

Uncle Harry beckoned to me to follow him. Embarrassed by what had just happened, panicked that Uncle Harry had caught me, and worrying over what he was going to do, I trailed him to the Virginia Militia's camp.

We sat down beside the campfire in front of his tent. "So... you've been here all along," Uncle Harry said.

I hung my head and looked at the flames.

"How could you do it, Josh? Your folks must be frantic!"

"Pa won't care. He hates me," I whispered.

"Speak up, I can't hear you."

I cleared my throat, which was beginning to ache. "I said, Pa hates me."

"Whatever gave you that idea?"

I told him then—about how Matt was Pa's favorite, that I was always in trouble with Pa—how no matter what I did, it was never good enough. I finished with the story about Bessy and the longrifle.

"I'm surprised at Matt," Uncle Harry said, "but let's take one thing at a time here. To begin with, your father and I have our differences, but I know him to be fair-minded. I seriously doubt that Matt is his favorite."

I started to protest, but he held up a hand for silence.

"Hold on. Is it possible, do you think, that he appears to favor Matt because he's more reliable... your pa can count on him?"

That word again.

"As for the longrifle, have you ever thought that your father's 'stinginess' isn't stinginess at all, but a need to be careful with his money? There's no life in the world any harder than a farmer's— particularly here, on the frontier." Uncle Harry paused to light his pipe. "I admire your pa more than anybody I know. Truth is, I'd trade places with him in a minute."

"But you're with the militia! You're not tied down to some silly old farm. You can come and go as you please—and you have so many friends... ."

He shook his head. "I'm like the rolling stone that gathers no moss. I've no wife, no family, no property to speak of—nothing of value to come home to. As for friends, Josh—friends come and go. Most of them, you can't count on."

I could hardly believe my ears. Uncle Harry had been my hero for as long as I could remember, yet here he was telling me that the very things I worshiped him for—his independence and popularity—weren't nearly so satisfying as Pa's life, which I had long ago decided was dull, a lot of hard work, and not for me.

"What are you going to do—about me?" I said, afraid of his answer.

He looked at me, his face more serious than I had ever seen it. "With the troops moving out, I'm restricted to the fort and can't leave to take you home. You'll have to come on to Fort Duquesne with the rest of us."

The fort hummed with activity next morning. Everyone laughed and joked as they began to pack up and break camp—lighthearted because the long wait was over and the march to Fort Duquesne was about to begin.

Grooming Ranger, I was wondering how the troops could

march without the supplies from Winchester, when Mister Alton walked up to me.

"Jed?"

"Yes sir, what can I do for you?"

"Doctor Franklin persuaded the State Assembly to buy food for the officers," he said. "A pack train has come in loaded with provisions. Thought you might like to come with me and help me bring back the captain's share."

"You bet," I said. I tethered Ranger and we set out together. Walking along, I asked, "What about the rest of the men?" As the captain's groom, I had plenty to eat—but from what Uncle Harry told me, I knew the enlisted men were grumbling about the lack of decent food.

He shrugged. "It's a pity about the men, but there's nothing we can do about it. Any help in their behalf will have to come from the general."

While Mister Alton haggled over what he felt Captain Washington should receive, I spent the time watching the men unload the horses. There were hams and cheeses, loaves of sugar and flasks of oil as well as kegs marked Raisins, Sturgeon, and Herrings and boxes of spices, pickles, and mustard. After unloading a barrel of potatoes and chests marked Lemons, the men uncovered kegs of biscuit and tubs of butter. The last things unloaded were a cask of vinegar and some kegs of spirits. The troops weren't going to like the fact that none of this food was for them.

A week passed. After all the preparations for a march, nothing happened. The general had changed his mind, but the redcoats and militiamen couldn't leave the fort.

I had done my other chores and was about finished grooming Ranger when Oliver came by.

"Glad to see you," I said. "Want to go hunting?"

"'Tis well for some, but ye don't have a gun."

"Maybe not, but I've got a weapon." I tethered Ranger where he could graze and pulled my sling out from under my belt.

"Can ye hit anythin' with that?"

73

I smiled and didn't answer. In the forest a few minutes later, I killed a squirrel.

"Brilliant!" Oliver said. "Do ye think I could learn?"

I was showing him how to swing the sling when an insect buzzed by my ear—then another and another. "C'mon, we'll do this later." I motioned to Oliver to follow.

I pushed my way through the dense vegetation. Every now and then, I paused and cupped a hand to my ear to listen. By the time Oliver caught up with me, I was standing near the trunk of a dead tree hollowed out by termites. It was humming with bees. Even from where we stood, we could see pounds of dark honeycomb filled with honey. Oliver licked his lips and ran toward it.

"Wait!" I called him back. "Let's do it like Pa does." I dropped to my knees and cleared a patch of dirt—then dug in my pouch for some lint left over from Ma's spinning. Mounding the lint on the space I had cleared, I fished in my pouch again and brought out a flint and a piece of steel. Sparks flew as I struck the stone against the metal. The lint began to smoke. Once I had a fire going, I dipped a green pine branch into the flames.

"Stay here," I said, "I'll be right back." Waving the smoking branch from side to side, I approached the beehive. The smoke quieted the bees. They left me alone while I stole some of their honeycomb. I brought it back to Oliver, and we hurried to our special rock.

"This is a bit of all right," Oliver said, chewing a piece of honeycomb.

Licking honey off my fingers, a thought inspired me. "I've been racking my brain, trying to figure out what to do about Willie…"

"And?"

"I want you to go back to camp and give him some of the honeycomb."

"Why ever would ye want to do that?"

I grinned, resisting the urge to blurt out my plan. "Don't tell him where it came from. Just let him know you're coming back for some more. If I know Willie, he'll follow you. Make sure he gets a

good look at the bee tree—then come back here. I'll handle the rest."
We finished our honey—all but what Oliver was taking to Willie—and parted company. I retraced my steps and hid in some bushes with a clear view of the bees' nest. It wasn't long before I heard the rustle of leaves. Oliver appeared and paused in front of the bee tree, stretched, and ambled off in the direction of the creek. I caught a glimpse of red through the thicket. Willie approached the bees—clearly thinking the honey was worth a sting or two. I armed my sling. When he was close enough to touch the honeycomb, I let fly the stone. My aim was perfect. It landed in the heart of the bees' nest.

Hundreds of bees boiled out of the hollow tree. Willie screamed and swatted as bees tangled in his hair and clothing and flew into his ears and nose. He tore through the trees, his face lumping with welts. Delighted that my plan had worked—a little worried it might have worked too well—I ran to tell Oliver.

"So what happened, lad—and don't ye spare the details," Oliver demanded as soon as I joined him on the rock.

Forcing a laugh, I told him about Willie being stung and how he had run away. The stings burning on the back of my own neck, I kept to myself.

"What do ye say, boyo—ye teach me how to use a sling, and I'll teach ye how to play the fife," Oliver said, his mouth full of chewy honeycomb. We had waited a while for the bees to settle down—then returned to their hive with another smoking branch and helped ourselves.

"Done!" I reached for his fife and placed it against my mouth—something I'd been itching to do ever since I first saw it. Pursing my lips, I began to blow. Oliver chuckled as a shrill toot sounded. It had looked so easy!

He took the fife and held it to his own mouth, showing me how to position my fingers over the holes while he tucked in his bottom lip and curled his top lip over. "Like this." He blew, and a firm well-pitched note sounded.

I tried again—this time with better results—and practiced a

while. When the lesson was over, I picked out a knothole for a target and began to teach Oliver how to use my sling.

"Try it again," I said, as he whipped a stone at the knothole for the umpteenth time and hit the sapling next to it. Little by little, he improved. "You'll get the hang of it," I told him. "Like you said about playing the fife, 'all it's goin' to take is practice.'"

On our way back to camp, Oliver poked me and said, "Who's that?"

"Where?"

"Over there... the man wavin'." He pointed to a group of militiamen.

I panicked as Uncle Harry broke away from his companions and came toward us.

"Josh—"

"Sorry, sir, you must be mistaken," I interrupted him.

Uncle Harry looked at me and then at Oliver. "Sorry," he said, "my mistake."

Oliver watched him walk away. "Sure ye don't know that fellow, Jed?"

"Never saw him before," I lied. "Why do you ask?"

"I'm not sure," he answered, a puzzled look on his face. "He reminds me of someone—but I can't think who."

CHAPTER NINE

TERROR AND TRIUMPH

Food was rationed more than ever. I kept my eye out for Daniel, but he and the other wagoners General Braddock had sent to Winchester for supplies hadn't come back.

"The general's beside himself over desertions and the men's complaints," Mister Alton said one morning after Captain Washington left the tent to attend yet another meeting.

"It might help if they had enough to eat," I answered.

"Jed!" a voice called.

Oliver! I stepped outside. "What's up?"

"A soldier from the 44th has been found guilty of thievin'. He's to get a thousand lashes and be drummed from the regiment with a halter about his neck. Want to—"

"Not me," I interrupted him before he could finish. "Nobody could survive that."

"Oh, he won't get them all at one time, boyo—but a hundred lashes a week."

I shook my head.

He thought about it. "You're right. I've no need to see that, either. Did ye see the order about gamblin'?"

"Where is it?" I asked, fear gripping me.

"I'll show ye."

He took me to where it was posted, and I read it aloud. "Any non-commissioned officer or soldier found gaming will immediately receive three hundred lashes without being brought to a court-martial. On-lookers to the gambling will be deemed equally guilty and receive the same punishment."

"See you later, Oliver." I took off running.

"Where're ye goin', boyo?" he yelled after me.

I wished I could tell him.

Just as I feared, Uncle Harry was in the middle of a card game, the cash he had won stacked in front of him. He and three other men were sitting on camp chairs around a big wooden box they were using for a table. They must have been playing a while. The air inside the tent was thick with tobacco smoke and smelled of rum.

Uncle Harry was looking at his cards. He didn't see me until a middle-aged man with brown hair and a scar on his cheek pointed at me and said, "You—get out of here. You don't belong."

"Josh!"

I knelt beside Uncle Harry and whispered, "We've got to go."

He waved me away. "Not now, Josh, I'm on a run."

"C'mon, Uncle Harry—before you get caught. The general's handed down orders that..."

"Stand and surrender! You're under arrest!" a loud voice commanded.

Uncle Harry dashed to the rear of the tent and slashed an opening in the canvas. "Josh! Come on!" he called and disappeared. Too late. The arresting soldiers had already rounded up the other gamblers, and I was among them.

"Where are they taking us?" I asked one of the gamblers.

"The stockade."

We were marched in bright sunlight through the gates of the fort to one of the log buildings I had seen when I first came to Fort Cumberland. The soldier in charge lined us up and wrote down our names—then he opened the door to a long, narrow room and locked us up.

It took my eyes a while to adjust to the dim light filtering through the window. There must have been ten of our colonists on one side of the room and the same number of redcoats on the other. Smelling their unwashed bodies, I barely managed a swallow. "Well, lookie here," a sandy-haired ranger in soiled buckskin said, pointing. He was sitting on the plank floor, as were most of the men. "Don't you recognize him?" The ranger nudged the man beside him. "He's the boy that squaw had her eye on." The man snickered. "And which eye was that?" The room rippled with laughter. I stared at the floor, hoping that in the darkness the men couldn't see the color I could feel warming my cheeks.

"Leave him alone," a low voice rumbled from the corner of the room and a bearded colonial I had never seen before stepped out of the shadows. "He's also the lad who started the riot a few weeks back. Beat the livin' hell out of that whey-faced redcoat that was pickin' on him."

The sandy-haired ranger's quarrelsome sneer turned to a look of approval. "You don't say! Then congratulations are in order on two counts."

A stocky redcoat jumped up and grabbed the ranger's tunic. As if on signal, the colonials and redcoats fell on one another, scuffling and punching and swearing. The door swung open. A guard threatened the men with his bayonet. The prisoners shuffled back to their places.

"You, boyo—come with me." The soldier motioned to me to follow.

I was marched through the fort, miserably aware of curious eyes watching. I could feel the blood pounding in my ears.

"They're taking the lad to Gage, for sentencing," an onlooker said, answering my unasked question. I thought of the bloody flogging I had witnessed with Oliver and my legs turned to jelly.

Colonel Gage was seated at his desk in the officer's quarters, his face stern. His cold eyes raked me up and down. "What have you to say for yourself?"

I couldn't answer.

"You are young to be gambling."

I clenched my teeth, determined not to betray Uncle Harry.

"How old are you?"

"T-thirteen, sir." I looked at the floor.

"Humph." There was a long silence. "You will have to suffer the consequences of your actions." Colonel Gage turned to his orderly. "Strip off his shirt and bring me my riding crop."

A whipping! My skin prickled and black spots appeared before my eyes.

"In deference to your age, I'll deliver the punishment myself—here in my quarters."

The sting of leather on my bare back was as terrible as I had imagined—the willow switch Pa had hit me with in the past a feather, by comparison. I bit through my lip, trying not to yell, as the whip lashed me a sixth time.

"What's this?"

I craned my head around and looked into Captain Washington's face.

"Jed?"

The colonel dropped the whip to his side. "You know this lad?"

"He's my groom. Why are you flogging him?"

Colonel Gage eyed me with distain. "He was arrested for gambling."

Ashamed that he should see me this way, I couldn't meet the captain's eye.

"Were you gambling, Jed?"

"No, sir." I swiped at my bleeding mouth with the back of my hand.

"Then what were you doing there?" Colonel Gage demanded.

I clenched my teeth and refused to answer.

Colonel Gage scowled at the captain. "He has to be punished. The general's orders state that—"

"I'm well aware of the way the general's orders read," Captain Washington interrupted him. "As I said, Jed is a member of my party. I know him to be an honorable lad. I am asking you to release him into my custody."

Colonel Gage glared at him, clearly angry that a mere captain would challenge his authority. Their gaze held for a long moment—until the colonel's eyes wavered. Tossing the riding crop aside, he snapped, "Very well. So be it."

With a curt nod, Captain Washington retrieved my shirt from the orderly and handed it to me. Fumbling, I pulled it on.

When we were on our way, I said, "How can I ever thank you, sir?"

"By causing no further trouble."

We walked to the edge of the encampment. I couldn't stop thinking about what had happened—the soldiers breaking up the gambling—Uncle Harry's escape and them catching me. Every time I thought about Colonel Gage, my eyes watered and my back stung. It was so unfair that I had been punished! I was angry with Uncle Harry for taking such a risk.

"How do you feel?" the captain asked.

I remembered what Lettie had said to Uncle Harry, in the face of all her troubles, and answered, "I'm fine, sir."

"Good, because I've a task for you. A mission." His voice was grave. "It's imperative I meet with Half King in secret immediately. John Alton is recognized throughout the garrison as my orderly, and I've no one else to send. I want you to go to Half King's camp and bring him to me."

Me? Captain Washington wanted me to bring the Seneca chief to him? I looked at him with amazement.

"With your hunting and fishing, you are more familiar with the outlying areas than I. Can you suggest a place for us to meet, away from prying eyes?"

My mind raced. "Yes, sir." I left the captain at Wills Creek, sitting on the rock Oliver and I had claimed for our own.

It felt wonderful to have been selected—but then I began think about what terrible things could happen if I made a mistake or forgot something important. Pa would have said I couldn't do the job and that I'd cause some awful disaster. Was he right? Could

I do it? Half King was a chief. Why would he listen to a boy like me? Would he remember me from the time when he and his braves teased me about my sling?

My heart pounded as I entered the Indians' camp. The air smelled foul. Children were playing with sticks and stones and rawhide dolls outside their wigwams. As I passed, they went quiet and stared. Braves stopped what they were doing to watch me. I recognized Half King's son. His eyes weren't teasing now! I needed directions and couldn't bring myself to ask.

I kept telling myself that Captain Washington wouldn't have sent me if it were dangerous. Finally I saw a squaw bending down feeding wood to a campfire. I walked over to her, my fingers crossed behind my back for luck. "Half King?" I said, hoping she understood.

The woman stood and turned around. She looked me up and down and grinned.

"Pretty boy!"

Bright Lightning! I wanted to run, but the captain was counting on me. I had to complete my mission. "Monacathothe?" I croaked.

Half King appeared in the doorway of the wigwam and waved her aside.

I gulped. "Captain Washington wants to see you, sir. Alone, at a special place. I'm to take you there."

I felt as if he was looking right through me. Then his eyes shifted to the sling hanging from my belt. He motioned for me to show him the way.

Careful, I thought, when we reached the woods that would take us to Wills Creek. I didn't want Half King to feel that I couldn't handle myself—and the captain didn't want anybody to know about this meeting. I kept thinking about the bear Daniel had to shoot, to save us, and cautioned myself with every step not to snap a twig underfoot or brush against foliage that might rustle.

As we approached the rock where Captain Washington was waiting, my fears began to ease. Half King grunted and pointed skyward and we stood there, admiring a pair of gray herons flying overhead. Suddenly, through the corner of my eye, I glimpsed a swaying of the marshy grasses. A water moccasin slithered out next to Half King's bare ankle, its mouth wide open and deadly. If I tried to warn him, he might move and the cottonmouth would strike! Quickly, I armed my sling and let fly. The snake recoiled, its head crushed, as Half King grabbed for his tomahawk.

He stared at the snake and then at me, his face unreadable. With a swift motion, he ordered me to move on.

I left Half King and Captain Washington standing on the rock beside Wills Creek. Braving a glance at the Seneca's face when I nodded goodbye, my heart skipped. Just for a second, I thought I saw a glint of approval in his flinty eyes.

I made my way through the brush and hurried to the fort. Uncle Harry would have no way of knowing what had happened to me since my arrest. I had to find him and tell him I was all right. I went to his tent, but he wasn't there. I asked several Virginia militiamen if they knew where he was, but they couldn't help me. I finally spied him standing at the entrance of Colonel Gage's quarters. He was shouting at the colonel's orderly.

"But I have to see him!"

I broke into a run. "Stop, Uncle Harry—don't say any more!"

Uncle Harry pivoted. I cringed when he hugged me, the stripes on my back still smarting from my whipping. The orderly shrugged and ducked inside the tent.

"Can't tell you how worried I've been!" Uncle Harry said, as we made our way to the Virginia Militia's camp. "They wouldn't let me into the stockade to see you, so I decided to go to Gage, himself. Thought, if I turned myself in, he might let you go."

"Sure glad I stopped you." I told Uncle Harry how Captain Washington had come to my rescue.

"A fine man—the captain," he said.

I wished I could tell him about my mission to the Seneca camp, how I'd taken Half King to see Captain Washington—about the snake and all—but it was a secret between the captain and me and I wasn't about to betray his trust, even with Uncle Harry..

"I never told Colonel Gage you were in that tent gambling," I said.

Uncle Harry smiled and put his arm around my shoulder.

After visiting Uncle Harry, I returned to Captain Washington's tent. Mister Alton was in a sour mood.

"General Braddock really botched it this time," he said.

"What happened?" I asked, surprised to find him so upset.

"Because of some problems we've had with the women, he's dismissed most of them from camp—including the Indians' wives."

"What's wrong with that, sir?"

Mister Alton frowned. "The braves are leaving to take their families home. They've promised to come back, but I don't believe it. Without them, we're going to be hard-pressed for guides and scouts."

That evening, after supper, Mister Alton saw me ease my sore back against a tree trunk. Captain Washington must have told him about the whipping, because he disappeared inside the tent and returned with a jar. "Here, son. This'll help." He had me take off my shirt and rubbed my welts with bear grease. The pain was better, but the smell made think of Bright Lightning.

When he finished, I put on my shirt and pulled out my journal to look at Lettie's rose. I really missed her. What if I wrote to her? Her mother had taught her to read and write just as Ma had taught Matt and Me. Miz Martin was from a gentle background too. That was one reason our mothers were such fast friends, Ma said. They had a lot in common.

I had no way to send a letter, but just writing down my thoughts would be like talking to Lettie. Maybe I'd show it to her some day. The blank pages made me a little nervous—but she wouldn't mind if it wasn't perfect. I took out my quill and ink.

Dear Lettie,

So much has happened since I saw you, I hardly know where to start. I had some more trouble with Matt and Pa. I'll tell you about it, when I get home. Anyhow, it was the reason I ran away.

Fort Cumberland isn't what I expected. The redcoats drill, while the men in the militia sort of mill around in their regular clothes, except for the officers. A lot of the folks here are hungry. General Braddock isn't giving them enough to eat. He blames everything on us colonials. He doesn't like us or our land!

Hardly any of the redcoats get along with us. Most of them are ready to pick a fight at the drop of a hat! But I've made one good friend. His name is Oliver. He's from Ireland. He's teaching me how to play the fife. You'd like him, Lettie. There isn't a mean bone in him.

The general sent my friend Daniel and some other wagoners to Winchester for supplies. I don't think we'll move out until they get back.

I've had some trouble here, but I'm trying hard to do better. I won't explain now, but I'm Captain Washington's groom. He has a good sense of humor, but I wouldn't want him for an enemy! I've found out another thing, Lettie. Indians still scare me, but they aren't all bad. I sort of did a favor for the Seneca chief. I'll tell you about it, when I see you.

More later.
Your friend,
Josh

CHAPTER TEN

THE CAMPAIGN

"Savages! We're bein' attacked!"

Oliver! Still half asleep, I jumped out of the wagon and found him waiting for me. The trees on the mountains surrounding the fort looked black against the dawning sky. We raced to the parade ground and scooted under a wagon. Whooping and hollering, a handful of Indians on horseback were waving their muskets and tomahawks.

"Heck, Oliver, those aren't enemies—they're Half King's braves!"

Just then, British regulars fired on them.

I watched helplessly as Half King's son and some other Senecas fell from their horses. "For gosh sake, your troops are killin' 'em!"

"Aw, no," Oliver groaned.

Later that morning, Mister Alton confirmed it. "The captain's in a temper. Those Indians were Half King's scouts. They were drunk because the redcoats gave them liquor, looking for some fun."

"What'll the general do?" I asked.

"My guess is—he'll post another order."

Sure enough. The order read: "If any soldier should dare to give strong liquor to the Indians, he is to be brought before a general court martial and tried for disobedience." As soon as I saw it, I breathed a thankful prayer that it hadn't been in effect when Uncle

Harry bribed Bright Lightning into letting me go.

I couldn't understand General Braddock's thinking. I had been at Fort Cumberland less than three weeks. During the time I had been there the general had commanded the troops to be ready to march on an hour's notice, days had passed and nothing had happened, keeping everybody on edge—and now the general was sending six hundred men to clear a road and build a fort and supply base at a place called Little Meadows—where the troops would rest on their march to Fort Duquesne. Shouldn't he have done that first? The good side, of course, was that militiamen weren't allowed to leave the fort, and Uncle Harry couldn't take me home.

A few days passed. It was early evening, when word buzzed through camp that the supply wagons were finally coming in. I ran to meet them, looking for Daniel.

"Dan'l—Dan'l Boone!" I saw him and waved.

"Jed!" he cried. "We're on our way to the commissary. Come help me unload."

I had finished my chores for Mister Alton. Daniel's wagon was moving slowly, in line with the others. I climbed up into it and sat down. Daniel looked tired, but he seemed glad enough to see me.

We drove through the gates of the fort to the parade ground. I helped him unload sacks of flour and other goods. Then he drove the wagon back to our camp and I set a campfire. Daniel brought out some jerky and biscuit and rum and we sat down beside the fire to visit.

"What took you so long, Dan'l?"

"Trouble roundin' up supplies. Folks didn't want to sell us their goods." He sipped his rum. "So, what did you do while I been gone?"

"I've been with Captain Washington," I said, trying my best not to sound prideful.

Daniel looked surprised.

"I—did him a favor. He asked me to take care of his gelding and gave me a place to stay."

"No wonder you look proud as a dog with two tails!" He

slapped me on the shoulder. "I should of known better'n to worry about you."

Daniel did care about me! He didn't hold a grudge over Buck, after all. I looked away so as not to show how pleased I was. "How was Winchester?" I asked.

"The Shawnees've been makin' trouble."

"What kind of trouble?"

"They've been poisonin' folks' wells with buckeyes." He reached inside his pouch and drew out a shiny brown nut shaped like a deer's eye.

I took it from him and rubbed it between my fingers. "These aren't poisonous. Squirrels eat 'em."

"They'll kill a man."

Just then a familiar voice called out, and Uncle Harry strolled into view. "There's my uncle," I said.

"Quick, into the wagon!"

When I didn't move, Daniel sat back and stared.

"It's all right, Dan'l—he knows I'm here."

"Well, I'll be." He scratched his head. "A lot's happened since I been gone."

I introduced the two men and Uncle Harry joined us beside the fire. "From what my nephew tells me, you saved his bacon when he first came to the fort," Uncle Harry said. "I don't know whether to thank you or not, because I could've taken him home—but I'm glad he landed in safe hands."

"He's a good lad." Daniel's eyes twinkled as he glanced in my direction. "Just had to chip off a few rough edges."

"Where're you from?" Uncle Harry asked.

"I was borned on the banks of the Delaware—about twenty miles north of Philadelphia—but North Carolina's home now."

"You a wagoner, ordinarily?"

"Naw—huntin' and trappin's more my line, but I needed a job and thought it might be interestin'."

"I'm afraid it's going to be a lot more than that." Uncle Harry stood up and looked at me. "Come see me in the morning, Josh and let me know what you decide to do."

"So that's your Uncle Harry," Daniel said, watching him walk away. "I might've known."

"What do you mean?"

"You're the spittin' image of him."

Could it be true? I always thought Uncle Harry was handsome. Another thought caught me up short. Was that the reason why Pa didn't like me—because I looked like Uncle Harry? I was turning the idea over in my mind, when Daniel said, "What're you goin' to do now?"

I had postponed making a decision about who to stay with until Daniel got back from Winchester. I really liked Daniel, but I liked Mister Alton and Captain Washington, too—and I owed them something. I owed all of them something. Without Daniel's help, in the first place, I probably would have been home by now.

The fact that Daniel was being so friendly made my decision all the more difficult. I was relieved when he said, "Why don't you stay with the captain? Takin' care of his horse is important. It don't mean we can't see each other."

Orders were issued for the 44th Regiment to be ready to march. The following afternoon, I discovered a swelling near Ranger's hoof. It was probably only an insect bite, but the captain should know about it.

"Captain Washington isn't here," Mister Alton said, when I asked for him.

"Where is he?"

"General Braddock wanted to talk with him in private before the council meets today."

I went looking for Oliver, and we headed for the creek.

"Ouch!" I fell to the ground and grabbed my foot.

"What is it?"

"My blasted shoe has a hole in it!" I pulled out a thorn, grabbed a handful of grass, and stuffed it inside my moccasin.

"If I didn't need 'em, I'd let ye have my shoes."

I looked at Oliver's long feet and grinned. "With those feet, you could just about sleep standing up!" He socked me and we tussled until we were out of breath. "C'mon," I said, "it'll be dark soon." Drums had beat retreat an hour ago, but the creek still shimmered in the setting sun.

"What's that noise?" Oliver said.

I cocked my head to listen. "A peeper. A tree frog. He's courting his sweetheart."

"You have one?"

"What, a frog?" I said, deliberately misunderstanding.

"I'll swear, Jed Beddington, ye're slippery as an eel! Not a frog—a sweetheart. You never did say."

How could I? If I told him about Lettie, I'd have to come up with a whole new set of lies—like where she lived and how I came to know her. To distract him, I reached for his fife and piped a tune.

He grinned. "Not bad, for a beginner." He picked up my sling and hit our knothole target just off-center.

"You're pretty good, yourself." I skipped a stone across the water. "How's Willie?"

"Just now out of infirmary. The bees had a grand way with him, Jed."

I felt a twinge of conscience. I never meant for Willie to be stung so badly.

"Maybe that's a lesson for us redcoats," Oliver said. "Ye colonists have a brilliant way of gettin' even."

The stars were coming out. Fireflies blinked among the trees. "We'd better get back to camp," I said.

We retraced our steps to the place where we usually parted, and I headed for the Virginia Militia's encampment.

Uncle Harry was sitting on a camp chair beside his tent, cleaning his longrifle. As soon as he saw me, he set the gun aside. "I'm glad to see you," he said. "I've been wanting to talk to you. There's something you should know, Josh." He cleared his throat. "Soldiering isn't easy under the best of circumstances. The way this campaign's started out, we may be in for a peck of trouble."

"How far is it to Fort Duquesne, anyhow?" I asked.

"A hundred and ten miles—but it might as well be five hundred."

"Is the road that bad?"

He nodded. Picking up his longrifle, he ran his hand over the wooden stock. "Look after yourself, Josh. I can't help feeling responsible for you." Grinning, he added, "And don't do anything your old uncle wouldn't do."

I smiled, hiding the nibble of fear I had come to associate with him. Uncle Harry was a risk taker. I'd found that out the hard way. I winced every time I thought about the colonel whipping me.

Colonel Halkett's 44th Regiment of British regulars and some militiamen left Fort Cumberland on the 8th of June—just two days shy of my being there a month. It was a grand sight, the redcoats marching in formation in their splendid uniforms to the beat of the drums and piping fifes.

Oliver's regiment was to leave in three days. I had hoped to see him before he left, but he was restricted to camp to get ready to march. Getting ready for the march myself, I checked my gear and discovered that some of the rawhide on my sling needed replacing. Changing it, I was reminded of Matt. He'd hate it, if he could see me now. What was he doing? Probably pulling boulders and trees out of that piece of land Pa wanted to plant. He and Pa could've used my help. I shrugged off a feeling of guilt.

When reveille sounded the next morning, I threw on my clothes to watch the main body of the militia move out. The sight was disappointing, after seeing the redcoats march the previous day. Except for officers, most of our men were dressed in anything they could find to put on their backs. I spied Uncle Harry, with the artillery and ammunition wagons—then Daniel, driving his supply wagon—and waved to them both, impatient to be on the road, myself.

Two days later, I checked my bundle one last time to make sure I hadn't forgotten anything. The 48th Regiment—and Oliver—would march this morning under the command of Colonel Dunbar. Mister Alton said the provision wagons, packhorses, oxen, and cows would follow them. The remaining women and sutlers would bring up the rear. The general and his staff, including us, would be the last to leave—followed by the baggage wagons. Mister Alton had been right. Hardly any Indians had come back after General Braddock ordered them to take their families home.

I rode with Mister Alton in Captain Washington's wagon. The day was sunny and clear—but hot and humid. My shirt was sticky with sweat.

Uncle Harry's fears about the march proved to be true. The advance party dispatched earlier to cut a road through the mountains had faced a near-impossible task. The road they had cut was barely passable—steep in many places and filled with rocks and freshly hacked tree stumps. Our horses grunted and blew, their mouths foaming, as they strained to pull the wagon.

We were only a couple of miles out of Fort Cumberland when the train came to a stop. Mister Alton jumped out of the wagon and held a hasty conversation with the driver in front of us. The man began to unhitch his team.

"What's he doing?" I asked, when Mister Alton returned.

"That's Savage Mountain, up ahead—named that for good reason. A Conestoga has halted at the bottom of the rise. They're afraid the wagon's too heavy to make it to the top. He's going to add his team to the other team to help them make the climb."

The double team strained to haul the Conestoga up the mountain, urged on by the crack of the driver's whip. At first, everything seemed all right. Then the front wheels began to lift. No! My heart raced as I watched the wagon tumble sideways and crash into the ravine, yanking the screaming horses to their deaths.

Mister Alton cursed. "You'd better get out and walk, son. You're added weight."

Shaken, I didn't know whether to be relieved or disappointed. I jumped clear of the wagon and watched our team pull it up the deadly rise. The lead horse stumbled! My breath caught as pebbles rolled down the road into the brush. Mister Alton steadied the team. I knew he was coaxing them forward with soothing words. Blowing hard, the horses made it to the summit.

I hardly slept that night, my muscles sore from the day's ride and my mind filled with nightmares about rumbling wagons and dying horses. Then something wakened me. I rolled over on my pallet and listened, my body tense. Ranger whinnied. I climbed out of the wagon and ran the few yards to where I had left him to graze.

The leather strap I had used to bind his front hooves together was gone! I had hobbled him. I was sure I had—well, almost sure. I rubbed Ranger's ears and slipped a rope around his neck. Then I tied the free end of the rope to my wrist and climbed back in the wagon.

In the morning, Mister Alton said, "You sleep all right, Jed?"

"No, sir, I didn't. Kept thinking I heard wagons. Toward morning, Ranger whinnied. I got up to see if he was all right." Feeling guilty, I said, "I don't know how it happened, sir, but his hobble was gone. I'm sure I hobbled him."

"I'm sure you did, Jed. Your quick thinking no doubt saved the bay from being stolen again. That was no idle thought about the wagons. A lot of civilian wagoners deserted last night, taking our horses with them. The road was more than they bargained for."

Alarmed by the desertions, General Braddock called the officers to a council of war. I overheard Captain Washington discuss it later with Mister Alton.

"I cautioned the general about the futility of trying to drag eight giant cannon over a hundred miles of man-killing mountain road," the captain said. "He's finding that what I said was true. The wagons are too heavy for the bad road and the sorry condition of the beasts we have to pull them."

"What are we going to do, sir?" Mister Alton asked.

"The general has ordered us to lessen the load on each wagon. Two six-pounders, four cohorns, and enough powder and stores to clear twenty wagons are to be sent back to Fort Cumberland. Inspect our personal supplies, John, and dispose of as much as you can."

"What about the stock?"

"Sentries will guard the horses as they graze in the woods at night. The horses are to be mustered and their numbers reported to the general each morning."

I debated with myself about revealing my ignorance. Curiosity won. When the captain left the tent, I asked Mister Alton, "What exactly is a cohorn?"

"A small mortar used to hurl grenades. They're pretty heavy, weigh some eighty-six pounds apiece."

Pa wouldn't have taken the time to explain. Encouraged, I said, "What's the difference between a six-pounder and a twelve-pounder?"

"Cannon are called after the size of the ball they can shoot. A six-pounder hurls balls that weigh just that—six pounds."

The train inched forward, through rugged mountains thick with trees and bushes. We traveled little more than three miles a day. I overheard Captain Washington complain to Mister Alton, "We halt to level every mole hill and to erect a bridge over every brook!"

When we finally dropped down into Little Meadows, it was dusk. The captain had a bad headache and fever. Mister Alton and I ate a bite of supper, and I took out my journal.

Dear Lettie,

We're finally on our way to Fort Duquesne! The road is awful. Today we traveled through woods called The Shades of Death! It took us nine days to get here and we only came 24 miles! It's really hot.

I'm worried, Lettie. Before we left the fort, I heard Daniel and Captain Washington arguing. The captain told the general we should split up our forces so our troops can reach Fort Duquesne before the French send reinforcements from Canada. He wants the general to leave the supply wagons behind. They slow down the march, he said. Daniel told him, if they do that, the men will soon be marching on empty bellies! I don't like it that they're arguing.

Captain Washington is sick. Probably from the water. A lot of the men are sick. I wish I had Ma's medicine box. I have a lot of tick sores and mosquito bites. I haven't had a chance to see Oliver or Uncle Harry since we left the fort.

I miss you.
Your friend,
Josh

CHAPTER ELEVEN

TOUGH DECISIONS

The last of the army trickled into Little Meadows, but I'd been too busy helping Mister Alton get ready for today's march to see Oliver or Uncle Harry. General Braddock had agreed with Captain Washington's suggestions. Most of the troops were going to push on. Colonel Dunbar was to stay at Little Meadows a few days—then follow the troops to Gist's Plantation with the supplies and wait there for us to return after our victory at Fort Duquesne.

I saddled Ranger before dawn and brought him around to the captain's tent, only to find him still abed. He was to have left with the first contingent this morning, along with Mister Alton and me.

"How's Captain Washington?"

"He has the bloody flux!" Mister Alton answered in a hushed voice.

Dysentery! The same cramping misery that had plagued Lettie's grandfather.

"The doctor wants him to bed down in the wagon and stay at the rear of the train—says, if he doesn't, he'll endanger his life," Mister Alton said.

In the flickering candlelight, I could see him wring out a cloth and place it on the captain's brow. Mister Alton's hands were shaking.

"You all right?" I asked.

He shook his head. "I've a touch of the fever myself."

"What are we going to do?" I whispered.

Captain Washington groaned. "Is that you, Jed?"

"Yes sir." I approached the bed.

"Find Boone," he murmured. "Go on with him. We'll come forward as soon as I'm able to ride." He motioned me away before I could answer.

The 44th Regiment and the Second Color of the 48th were already in place and ready to march. I hurried to get my bundle out of Captain Washington's wagon. By the time I reached the edge of the parade ground, the drums and fifes had started playing and the troops were moving out.

I looked for Oliver as the Second Color marched by—saw Willie first. I almost hollered to him something about honey, but my heart wasn't in it. Revenge wasn't as sweet as I had expected. Oliver saw me and nodded—never missed a note—and marched right by me.

I left the parade ground in search of Daniel. He was in line with the other supply wagons, waiting to pull out. "Dan'l!" I broke into a run.

He spotted me and waved. "What're you doin' here?" he asked, when I reached him.

"The captain's sick," I gasped. "Can I come with you?"

He smiled. "Suit yourself."

I threw my bundle into the wagon and climbed aboard, glad to be with him. With the train stretched out for miles along the narrow road, I knew my chances of spending time with Oliver or Uncle Harry would be slim.

We covered eight miles before coming to ground and making camp. News buzzed through the train that Half King had been captured earlier in the day. John brought Daniel the details.

"Half King was reconnoiterin' when he and his braves was ambushed. The French wanted to kill him on the spot, but another Seneca who'd thrown in with 'em talked 'em into settin' him free."

"How'd he manage that?" Daniel asked.

"He convinced 'em that Half King would come back and scare us with stories about how strong they are. They interrogated him fer hours about the size of our army and the kind of artillery we're carryin'."

"Did he tell 'em?"

"He did, but they didn't believe him. They said it wasn't possible to haul artill'ry through a country like we been through."

Daniel grunted. "They're not far wrong."

The drums signaled the men to rise at three o'clock next morning. They marched at five. We covered eight miles by late afternoon and made camp. I was starving. Huntsmen brought in venison and bear every day—but only for the officers. The rest of us had to make do with salt horse and biscuit.

Daniel picked up his longrifle. "I'll get us some game."

"I thought we couldn't fire arms within two miles of camp."

"Braddock changed the orders."

"Can I invite Oliver to eat with us?"

"All right with me—if you can find him."

He disappeared among the trees, leaving me to gather wood and set a fire.

Finding Oliver wasn't as difficult as I had supposed. I spotted his red hair less than a mile from the place where Daniel and I had camped.

"Oliver! Cunningham!"

"Jed!" He ran toward me, a big smile on his face.

"You wouldn't be interested in some fresh roasted meat in a while..." I teased.

"Oh, wouldn't I just." His eyes gleamed. "Are ye serious?"

"I can almost guarantee it. Dan'l's gone hunting."

He grinned. "Then it's a sure thing." But he hung back.

"What's wrong?"

"It's Willie. He's sick."

"He looked all right when I saw him three days ago."

"He's had the flux. It came on sudden-like." Oliver hesitated.

"Do ye think it'ud be all right if I brought him along?"

If Willie came, maybe I'd stop feeling guilty about what I did to him. "Go get him," I said. "I'll wait for you."

Willie's appearance shocked me. Difficult as the march had been, even for the healthy, I couldn't help feeling sorry for him.

"I apologize, Jed," he mumbled when he saw me, "—for everythin'."

Oliver motioned to me behind Willie's back, and I held out my hand.

"I reckon we're even now," I said.

Daniel had a brace of squirrels on the spit by the time we reached the campfire. John was with him. It was almost like old times.

"Better enjoy this, boys," Daniel said. "No tellin' when we'll have any more."

The meat roasting over the open fire set my mouth to watering, but I made myself hold back until the others had served themselves. We bolted down the first fresh meat any of us had eaten since we had left Fort Cumberland.

Before Oliver and Willie left, I beckoned Willie aside. He'd been quiet most of the evening.

"Sorry you got so many stings," I said. "I didn't mean for you to get sick."

Without his belligerent attitude, Willie looked pathetic.

"About the fight, Jed—I knew ye didn't knock me down on purpose. I was just showin' off."

On my pallet that night, I thought about Willie. We'd never be friends—not like Oliver and me—but at least we weren't enemies now. Something inside me released itself and I felt better. My thoughts turned to Matt. Would the time ever come when we could make peace? When Lettie came to mind a strange, painful sort of yearning to see her swept over me.

The train halted while sappers cleared the road ahead. It took us several days to reach Great Meadows, which turned out to be acres of grass parched by drought. We made camp a couple of miles beyond Fort Necessity, which lay in the middle of it. I unhitched the team, rubbed them down, and went on the hunt for Oliver.

"Want to go back and have a look at the fort?"

"Brilliant!" he said, his eyes gleaming.

There was little left of Fort Necessity to see. In the year since Captain Washington's surrender, the French had pulled down the log walls and torn apart the artillery pieces mounted in them. Oliver and I found bits of them rusting in the trench surrounding the fort. In my mind's eye I tried to place the captain and Uncle Harry here at this lonesome, deserted place with a hundred men, trying to defend it against so many of the enemy.

"Look!" Oliver pointed to a hollow-eyed skull.

Glancing around, I could see other human bones scattered among the weeds. We just stood there, quiet—staring at them.

"Would ye do somethin' for me?" Oliver asked.

"Name it."

"If anythin' happens to me, will ye let Tibby know?"

His request made me uneasy. "Nothing's going to happen to you, Oliver."

"Promise," he said. "She lives at thirty-two Paddington Lane in Cork."

"I promise." I wished he would change the subject.

"Give me the direction, so I know ye know it."

Squirming, I repeated it.

An owl hooted in the distance. Indians were superstitious— thought the call of an owl meant somebody was going to die. I glanced at Oliver, wondering if he knew that.

We returned to camp and Oliver went back to his regiment. The evening sky was clear, no promise of rain. I went to our wagon and fished in my bundle for my quill and ink—then settled myself against the wagon wheel and pulled out my journal.

Dear Lettie,

We finally got to a place called Great Meadows. To tell you the truth, I spend half the time bored and the other half scared to death! The rangers tell terrible stories about Indians and scalping, trying to scare the redcoats. But it's not all bluff. Yesterday a bunch of Indians attacked some of the wagoners. One of them took four musket balls in the belly! He had a hard time dying, Lettie.

The food is horrible, what there is of it. I don't know what I'd do, if it wasn't for Daniel. Sometimes, I wonder if life with Pa and Matt wasn't better than this. Did I make a terrible mistake, running away?

I'm not the only one feeling down. Daniel doesn't say much, but I can tell the delays and the general's mistakes that cause our folks to suffer are wearing on him.

I think about you a lot.

Your friend,

Josh

CHAPTER TWELVE

FINAL DAYS

The train crept four miles over a rugged mountain thick with trees and halted to set up camp in a clearing at the base of a rocky hill. Dozens of campfires lay scattered about, wisps of smoke still rising from some of them.

"The French and their Injuns just camped here," Daniel said. "By the look of things, must of been a couple a hundred of 'em." He picked up his longrifle. "Let's find John and go huntin'."

A chill rippled up my spine. "What about the Indians?"

Daniel grinned. "Long gone by now. C'mon, we'll find us some game. I don't know about you, but bread and half a pint of beans ain't my idea of a day's rations."

We located John and wound our way through the forest. Suddenly, something caught my eye.

"Look! Over there."

Tree after tree had been stripped of bark and painted with red pictures. I approached the closest one and traced a stick figure scalping a man.

Daniel dropped to his knee. "Whoa, John, look at this." There were two sets of tracks going off in different directions. "The Injuns've split up."

We returned to camp to report our findings to General Braddock. John volunteered to go with Captain Dobson and some seventy others to Redstone Creek and try to find out what was going on. The men were issued two days' rations: a biscuit and a gill of rum. The general offered a bounty of five pounds for every Indian scalp brought into headquarters.

The train continued its northward march, threading its way over a long, steep tree-covered mountain before dropping into a valley where a dozen crude cabins lay.

"What's that place, Dan'l?"

"Gist Plantation. The supply wagons're supposed to follow us here and wait fer us to get back after the battle. You heard of the Gists?" he asked.

"They're scouts," I said. "Christopher and his son, Nat. Pa used to talk about 'em."

"Chris saved Washington's life two times last year, when the colonel—er—captain was on his way back from the Ohio Valley."

"I didn't know that." Reminded of the captain, I wondered how he and Mister Alton were getting along. I hoped they were better. There was no way of knowing until they showed up. I leaned over the side of the wagon and looked at the dirt slipping past beneath the wheels. "Soil here looks like it would grow just about anything."

Daniel had heard my complaints about farming. "I'll swear, if you're not a born farmer," he teased.

If anybody had told me that seven weeks ago, before I left home, I would have taken it as an insult. Now, I wasn't so sure.

It started to rain during the night—a warm, soaking rain that drummed against the canvas wagon cover, seeping through the smallest holes until Daniel and I were drenched and miserable. By morning, the rain had turned into a regular gully-washer.

The freshly hacked road oozed with mud that stuck to the horses' hooves. Moving in line with the other wagons, we passed a number of dead horses lying by the side of the road.

"For gosh sake," I said, "I know there hasn't been much forage, but some of those horses look like they've been shot!"

Daniel hawked and spat. "It's them lyin' thieves that contracted with the army. They searched the country fer horses that were old and broken down and bought 'em fer a pittance—then turned 'round and sold 'em to Braddock fer a profit. Some of these horses just plain keeled over and died in their traces. Those with the musket balls in 'em broke down and had to be shot."

Captain Dobson and the volunteers who had gone with him to Redstone Creek caught up with the train at sundown, half a mile from the Youghiogheny River which Daniel said we'd have to cross again tomorrow.

It had been an awful day. It had been an awful few days, the train moving slow as molasses and hardly anything to eat. I was glad, when John showed up.

"See any Injuns?" Daniel asked, sipping his ration of rum that General Braddock had issued to all the men for what he called "good behavior."

"Nary a man, woman, or child. Them Injuns is on their way to join the French."

The skies were still overcast next morning, but no rain fell as we crossed the Youghiogheny River a second time. We scanned the hills looking for signs of Indians, but the trees and bushes were so thick we couldn't see much of anything.

The horses were dying so fast there weren't enough to draw more than half the supply wagons. Daniel said that as soon as we came to ground that afternoon the wagon master would be sending horses back for the wagons left behind. I hoped that Buck wouldn't be one of them. I liked both of the horses that made up our team— but Buck was special to me. The thought of sending him back to pull another heavy load was worrisome. Buck was already dragging from working so hard and from having so little to eat.

"I warned Captain Washington about the supplies not keepin' up with the troops," Daniel grumbled. "Men can't keep up their strength on three-quarters of a pound of flour and half a pound of bacon a day."

The horses weren't the only ones in trouble.

The following morning, we headed northwest over the rugged

mountains, traveling mile after dreary mile hemmed in by the woods and pestered by hungry insects. The day was clear. Another hot one.

"Only sixteen miles to Fort Duquesne now, by horse," Daniel said, after we made camp. "Half King's son and another brave've ridden out to reconnoiter." He left the wagon to visit with John.

I decided to walk and stretch my legs. The usual hum of conversation among the men after a march was missing. They were hungry. My stomach growled. I was hungry — and tired. At least I got to ride in a wagon instead of marching all day with a lot of heavy gear.

Most of the men were stretched out on the ground or leaning against tree trunks as they waited for the Indians' report. All of a sudden a ripple of excitement buzzed through the train, and I saw Daniel loping toward me.

"What is it?" I hollered, relieved that something — no, anything was happening.

He grinned. "A bunch of oxen're comin' in — must be a hundred of 'em — and wagons loaded with flour. Dunbar came through with provisions!"

General Braddock suspended his order about fires. A layer of smoke hung in the air as the men roasted the first meat we had been issued since we left Fort Cumberland.

The next morning, Half King's son and the Indian who had gone out scouting with him returned with a French scalp and presented it to the general. John heard the story first-hand and repeated it to Daniel and me.

"Our Injuns spotted him in a canoe. When he came ashore, they shot and scalped him. But they made a hasty job of it, thinkin' the enemy was near." He grinned. "They had to skin the durn thing again, to make it fit enough fer the general to look at."

My stomach churned, and I turned away. An hour later, we received word that some French Indians had attacked the rear baggage wagons and scalped a woman and soldier. I could see why they'd want to kill a soldier, but a woman? Daniel explained that to the Indians, killing a woman or child was considered courageous because it proved the warrior had come into the heart of enemy country.

Shortly after noon, news spread through the train that Indians had fired on our right flank. Half King's braves came to our rescue again—but in the confusion, the redcoats mistook them for French Indians and fired on them. Two warriors had been wounded. Half King's son had been killed. They brought his body back to the train in a wagon and the drums called the men to assemble for a special service.

I searched the crowd, looking for Oliver. Spotting his red hair, I waved. "Cunningham! Over here!"

He turned at the sound of my voice and ran toward me. "We bungled again," he said as we waited for the services to begin.

"It's not your fault, 'though I'm beginning to understand why Dan'l feels the way he does about redcoats—in general, that is." I didn't want Oliver to feel my criticism was directed at him.

Half King's son was given a Christian burial. An honor guard fired muskets over his grave while Half King cried out his grief to the Great Spirit because his son had been killed by one of us and not an enemy. Watching him, I couldn't help thinking about Pa. Would he grieve, if something happened to me? Ma would. What about Matt? Would he be sorry for all the things he did to make my life miserable?

When the train came to ground that evening the troops had marched ten miles, by Daniel's reckoning. We covered only half the distance the following day, because the guides got lost trying to avoid some swamps. We were running out of water. Scouts found some half a mile away, but it wasn't fit to drink.

Riding along in the wagon, I took stock of my situation. We were short of water, had almost no food, and the mosquitoes and wood ticks had just about eaten me alive.

"What's the date today?" I asked Daniel

"The eighth of July."

Two months since Matt let Bessy get out. Ma's vegetable garden would be full of good things to eat now. Carrots and squash, green beans and tomatoes.... My mouth watered.

"Braddock says if the Injuns try to stop us, it'll be at the river crossin' tomorrow on our way to the fort," Daniel said.

Just then, a wagon rumbled past, a bay trailing along behind. Ranger! Mister Alton was driving the team. The captain was seated beside him. His normally ruddy face looked pale.

"Captain Washington... Mister Alton... it's me, Jed!" I hollered.

"We're on our way to the head of the train, to report to General Braddock," Mister Alton called back. "Come and join us, when you can."

I looked at Daniel to see his reaction, but his face was unreadable. I didn't know what to do. I liked Daniel a lot, but he was a wagoner. Tomorrow, Captain Washington would be in the thick of things. I wanted to be with him.

It was almost dark when we finally made camp. Daniel hadn't said a word about me leaving. We shared what food we had, and I made a difficult choice. I knew all along, it was the right one. Daniel had been my first friend at the fort. He saved me from turning myself in to Uncle Harry and never let on that I was a runaway. And he hardly ever got impatient with me, like Pa did, when I made a mistake. "I'll be riding with you tomorrow, Dan'l."

He smiled. "Glad to have you aboard."

I went to where the 48th Regiment was camped and found Oliver.

"Not much sleep tonight," he said. "We're to parade in the mornin' at two o'clock and meet Colonel Gage's party at Frazer's Plantation."

I squirmed at mention of the colonel. I had never told Oliver about the whipping. How could I, and not tell him about Uncle Harry?

"Wish I had a musket," Oliver said.

"Me, too." For the first time in a long time, I thought about the longrifle I had found hidden in the hayrack at home.

Oliver and I said goodbye and I wandered the train, looking

for Uncle Harry. Things had changed between us since the guards caught me trying to stop him from gambling. I didn't admire him so much. But tomorrow we were going to war, and Uncle Harry was family. I wanted to see him.

I found him leaning against a wagon wheel, a cup in his hand. He was talking to a ranger. He beckoned me over as soon as he saw me and finished what he had been saying. "I understand Washington had to beg Braddock to let him lead tomorrow's charge."

"From all I hear, he's still feeling poorly," the ranger said.

"Sick or well, I'd rather be under the captain than anybody else." Uncle Harry took a sip of what had to be rum. "We're short of scouts. Braddock never should have sent the squaws home and risked losing the braves."

The ranger nodded. "We're down to eight now—no—seven, since they killed Half King's son."

"More like five," Uncle Harry said. "Two of them are wounded."

The ranger noticed me standing there. "Good night, Harry— and good luck tomorrow." With a nod in my direction, he went on his way.

Uncle Harry motioned to the fire and we sat down beside it.

"I came to say goodbye, Uncle Harry."

He scowled. "I hate it that you're here, Josh," he muttered. "I wish I could have taken you home. War can be a living hell."

Remembering his experience with Captain Washington, my heart went out to him. "You learned that at Fort Necessity, didn't you?"

He nodded, his face somber as he stared at the fire.

"Don't worry about me, Uncle Harry. I'll be fine."

He downed the last of his rum.

Finally, I said, "I've got to go." I stood up, reached out a hand, and pulled him to his feet. We hugged and said our goodbyes. I left him and walked to Captain Washington's tent, feeling uneasy.

"The captain's resting up for tomorrow," Mister Alton murmured, so as not to disturb him. "Put your things in the wagon."

"I'm staying with Dan'l," I whispered. "Thanks a lot, Mister Alton—for everything. I appreciate how you've been so good to me."

He smiled. "It's been a pleasure having you around, son. I'm sorry you're leaving us, but I know you have other ties."

"Please tell the captain goodbye for me—will you? And thank him for me? I hope he's feeling fit to ride tomorrow."

I held out my hand—but he grabbed me and hugged me. He cleared his throat. "I'll look for you after the battle."

I left the captain's tent and ran back to Daniel's wagon, trying my best not to step on anything sharp. I had thrown my moccasins away weeks ago and was barefoot.

Daniel was gone—probably visiting with John. I stretched out on my pallet inside the wagon, certain I'd never get to sleep. The next thing I knew, Daniel was shaking me by the shoulder.

"Rise and shine, Jed. Time to go to war!"

It was five o'clock. The drums were beating, signaling the men to form ranks.

I wondered how the general expected them to form ranks in a narrow road surrounded by trees and laurel slicks—but I didn't say anything. My stomach growled. I was hungry, but I didn't say anything about that, either. I wasn't sure there was anything to eat.

"Gage left with an advance party and two cannon before daybreak to clear the road for us," Daniel said.

I looked at the sky. "It's going be a clear day."

"And hot as blazes!"

The heat didn't phase the bugs. I batted at a cloud of gnats flying around my head and scratched a mosquito bite until I drew blood.

The train inched along. The road the colonel's men had cut through the forest was hardly a road at all. We halted mid-morning. The men pulled out their food—those who had any.

"Here, Jed, have some of this."

Daniel handed me a hunk of jerky and halved it with his skinning knife.

"Thanks," I said, savoring its salty toughness.

It was noon by the time we wheeled up to the Monongahela

River crossing. Along the shore, I could see campfires burning. Abandoned spears littered the area.

"Gage's men must've startled some redskins," Daniel said.

"Look at those spears!"

"Help yourself, Jed, but watch out fer the points. I wouldn't put it past them blasted Injuns to dip 'em in poison."

I jumped to the ground and picked up two spears—one for Oliver, who would have marched by in formation and not had a chance to get one—and one for me. Hesitating, I picked up a third spear for Matt. Like it or not, he was still my brother.

The Monongahela was knee-deep most places and hundreds of yards across, with a view up-river for several miles. The ground leading to the water was level, with very few trees. The train waded the river, marched a couple of miles, and prepared to cross it a second time.

"Why in the world do we have to cross the Monongahela again?" I complained. "Seems to me things are hard enough without crossing every river twice."

Daniel shrugged. "Franklin warned the general to stay away from narrow spots that could be dangerous."

"Why?"

"We don't want to get ambushed."

Fording the river wasn't difficult, but there was a steep bank on the far side of the second crossing we had to climb. Daniel let out a stream of oaths. Colonel Gage's men had attempted to slope the bank, but it was still all but impassable.

"Isn't this the place you told me about—where the general said we might be attacked?" I asked.

"It is." Daniel eyed the terrain, his longrifle within reach between us.

Men began to work on the bank. Time passed. I looked at the sun, impatient to be underway. "We've been here at least two hours, Dan'l!"

He nodded. "And no attack—even though we're sittin' here like ducks on a pond, invitin' one. I can hardly believe it, but it

111

looks like the French're goin' to give up without a fight, after all."

There was no sign of trouble when the soldiers at the front of the line finally climbed the embankment. They hooted and hollered and passed back word that the French had abandoned Fort Duquesne. The train quickened its pace to reach Frazer Plantation and meet with Colonel Gage's men, as planned.

The plantation had been torched! My thirst for war returned at the sight of another settler's home destroyed. Those goldarn French and their blasted Indians!

The train halted, awaiting further orders.

"Take care of things," Daniel said. "I'll see if I can find out what's goin' on." He jumped to the ground and headed for the plantation.

I spent the time grooming the team—especially Buck. "Poor thing," I whispered in his ear while I brushed him. "This will soon be over. The general said defeating the French shouldn't take more than three or four days."

Daniel returned with news. "Braddock decided not to strengthen our flanks 'cause the dangerous passes he was worried about are behind us. The train's goin' to move on. Gage and his men will stay just ahead of us."

I could hear the fifes and drums begin to play the grenadier's march—a merry tune I was familiar with because Oliver had taught it to me. In high spirits, the soldiers and wagons moved forward.

"Tarnation!" Daniel exploded a few minutes later.

I followed the direction of his pointed finger. There—pulled to the side of the makeshift road, were the two six-pounders Colonel Gage had brought across the river.

"What in hell does Gage think he's doin'?" Daniel sputtered.

"What do you mean?"

"Those cannon was our ace in the hole—the one thing those damn Injuns are afraid of."

We proceeded about a mile, Daniel cussing all the way. Then we heard a shout from the head of the train, "The Indians is upon us!" followed by savage screams and gunfire.

Daniel jumped to the ground, grabbed the harness, and cut the traces on the horses. Then he leaped into the wagon and hastily gathered up his things.

"What're you doing?" I cried.

"I know when a hog's fat. C'mon, we're ridin' out of here!"

I looked at him in disbelief. "Not me!"

"Suit yourself. Them redcoats don't know what they're doin'. It's gonna be a massacre!" He swung himself onto Buck's back and rode into the woods.

I hit the ground running and headed for the front of the train.

CHAPTER THIRTEEN

HORRORS OF WAR

I ran along the edge of the road toward the battle—the rocks and thorns ripping my feet, the ricochet of musket balls pinging in my ears. Soon I was caught in a tangle of men and wagons and frantic horses muddled together.

"You! Where's your weapon?" a voice pierced the deafening turmoil. I held out my sling and the ranger cried, "Get the devil out of here!"

The road was flanked by steeply sloping hills. I pushed my way up an embankment, through trees and bushes and trailing vines and reached the hilltop—then climbed an oak, gasping for breath. Looking down, I had a clear view of the narrow road below. It was a perfect spot for an ambush.

With mounting horror, I watched the French and their Indians hug the ground and dart from cover to cover—all of them naked from the waist up and splashed with war paint. They hardly had to aim their muskets to hit the uniforms I had so admired. Huddled together, twenty and thirty men deep, the redcoats were giant targets.

General Braddock galloped into the fray leading a detachment, his black gelding sleek with sweat. Militiamen were close behind, followed by more redcoats. The air was thick with black smoke.

The militia broke ranks, taking cover behind bushes and trees.

Stricken, I watched man after man in buckskin fall as the panicked redcoats fired aimlessly into the forest. Uncle Harry! I caught sight of him running up the hill across the way before he disappeared

Every time I saw General Braddock, he was on a different mount, shouting commands to charge the Indians on higher ground. The redcoats advanced and retreated—advanced and retreated. Each time, they were beaten back.

Ranger! The beautiful gelding wheeled and turned as Captain Washington rallied the colonial troops who hadn't taken cover in the woods.

"RANGER!" Blood spurted as a musket ball ripped a hole in the gelding's neck. Captain Washington leaped free of him, and the bay fell heavily on his side. Mister Alton ran to the captain and thrust him the reins of another mount.

I gnawed my lip, cursing the fact that I didn't have a gun.

Urged on by their officers, the redcoats advanced and fell back one last time—then the Indians swooped out of the forest, whooping their war cries and waving tomahawks. The redcoats broke ranks—started to run—throwing down everything that might slow them down. The back of my neck prickled as cries of the wounded and screams of those being tomahawked pierced the air. Clinging to the oak tree, I felt truly alone—with no one to rely on but myself.

At last, all was quiet. The French and their Indians must have gone someplace to celebrate. I had to find Oliver and Uncle Harry! Grabbing a limb, I swung to the ground and hurried down the slope to the road—passing heaps of bodies as I looked for something to identify the 48th Regiment.

There! I spied the colors of Oliver's company, trampled on the side of the road next to some dead redcoats. I rolled body after body over, looking at their faces—then stumbled backwards, stunned by the sight of Willie's dead eyes staring at me. I hesitated—then closed them and continued my frantic search for Oliver.

Indians had killed the wounded unable to flee. No sign of Oliver. I leaned against a tree, trying to decide what to do.

A groan drew my attention. I hurried toward a slick of mountain laurel bordering the road and shoved the branches aside. Oliver lay crumpled among the leaves. Sinking to my knees, I cradled his head in my lap, trying not to stare at the dreadful wound in his chest. His eyes fluttered. "Jed... ." He tried to smile. "I... hid in the bushes, like Dan'l said. Knew ye'd come... . Tell Tibby... I... loved..."

"No, Oliver, you're going to be fine!"

He coughed, and blood oozed from the corners of his lips. "Thirty... two... Kensington..."

"I remember."

He swallowed. "Ye... know..."

I nodded. "Tabitha Boggs. I'll write her, soon as I can."

"Want ye to have... me fife..."

I nodded again and swiped at the tears running down my cheeks. "One... more... thing... . Take..." his voice faltered.

"Take what?" I bent closer, trying to hear.

"Me... shoes. Ye... need... 'em." He sighed and was gone.

I sat back on my haunches, unable to move. Then reason returned. Oliver's body! I glanced around for a place to hide it. The Indians would be back, looking for booty and taking more scalps. They wouldn't have a chance at Oliver's red hair, if I could help it!

I spied a hollow in the slope of the hill and dragged Oliver to it—trying not to think about what I was doing. At the last minute, I hesitated—took off his shoes and laced them on my feet—then reached for his fife and stuck it in my belt. I concealed Oliver's body as best I could with vines and uprooted bushes and headed to the place where I had last seen Uncle Harry.

"Merciful Father, you can't take them both," I pleaded, running. "Please, God—if Uncle Harry's there, let me find him and let him be all right!"

I came to a clearing. An Indian! Panicked, I glanced around looking for others. He appeared to be alone. He leaned down, over a body, his tomahawk clutched in his fist. The bronze hand lifted...

"NO!" I shrieked.

The tomahawk stopped mid-air. The redskin looked at me as I swung my sling. A dribble of blood leaked from his temple, and he slumped to the ground unconscious.

I ran to the Indian's victim. Uncle Harry! There was a cut over his right eye and blood seeped from a wound in his shoulder, but he was breathing. "Uncle Harry! Wake up, Uncle Harry!"

"J-Josh? That you? Can't see... something wrong... ." His eyes closed again.

"C'mon, Uncle Harry—move!" I pulled him to his feet. Quietly as possible, I guided him through the woods. There were bodies along the river and floating in it. I retched as a woman bobbed against me in the blood-tinged water, her shiny skull covered with flies.

The retreat was so hasty, the survivors had abandoned every-thing: weapons, ammunition, wagons, and baggage. Those of us who had survived marched through the night—losing our way in the darkness and finding it again when the guides came upon hatchet marks they recognized on trees lining the road. The groans and cries of the wounded were a living nightmare.

The sun was just coming up. We were still marching, when I heard someone call my name.

"Jed—that you, Jed?"

Mister Alton's voice! I nearly cried.

"Been looking for you. I'd about given up." He put Uncle Harry's other arm around his shoulder, easing my load. "Thought you were with Boone."

"He left when the battle started," I said bitterly.

"All the wagoners did."

We paused to rest, and I introduced Mister Alton and Uncle Harry. If he was surprised by the news I had an uncle with the campaign, Mister Alton didn't show it. He looked at the cut over Uncle Harry's eye and fished inside his pouch for a clean rag.

"General Braddock had four mounts shot out from under him," he said, winding the cloth around Uncle Harry's head. "He was mounting his fifth, when he was wounded. He's in a litter, up ahead—in bad shape." He snorted. "Those redcoats are really something. It was all the general could do to muster six men to carry him."

"What about Captain Washington?" I asked.

"Sick as he is, he took command and covered the retreat after the general's other aides were wounded. He lost two mounts and took four bullets—fortunately through his coat."

"I saw Ranger go down."

Mister Alton sighed. "Too bad about the bay." Frowning, he said, "Braddock ordered the captain to ride to Colonel Dunbar to ask him to send provisions and hospital stores to Gist Plantation. They should be there when we arrive."

At least something to look forward to.

We marched all night and two more days, with nothing to eat and nothing to drink but fetid water. Uncle Harry's face was flushed with fever. He rarely spoke.

"It's the musket ball in his shoulder," Mister Alton said. "You need to get him to a surgeon, so he can remove it."

"Where is there a surgeon?" I asked, bone weary and worried.

"There should be one with Colonel Dunbar."

The fourth evening after the battle, what was left of the army trickled in to Gist Plantation, desperate for the food and supplies Colonel Dunbar was to have sent—only to learn the wagons hadn't arrived.

"What happened?" Mister Alton asked a passerby.

"Too many wagons and not enough horses to pull 'em."

"Where is Dunbar?" Mister Alton said.

"Eight miles south of here."

Exhausted, we slumped down under a hickory tree—Uncle Harry's out-stretched body between us.

"John Alton?" A bearded man in buckskin stepped out of the dusk.

"Micah! What're you doing here?" Mister Alton turned to me and said, "He's with the Virginia Militia."

"Captain Washington's still at Dunbar's camp," the man said.

"He's sick, John. The fever's come on him again. He sent me to fetch you."

Mister Alton struggled to his feet. "I'm sorry, Jed, but my first duty lies with the captain. Fever can kill, sure as musket balls."

"It's all right, Mister Alton. Don't worry about us... we'll be fine." Inside, I was shaking. It didn't take a doctor to see that Uncle Harry was getting worse.

When Mister Alton left, I pulled Uncle Harry to his feet and walked him to one of the cabins—then knocked, willing the settler to open the door.

The door squeaked open and a man with a longrifle stepped out, a plain middle-aged woman by his side.

"What do you want?" the man said gruffly.

"My uncle's hurt."

"So's just about everybody." The settler's eyes went from Uncle Harry's bloodstained tunic to the makeshift bandage around his head. "Sorry. Can't help you."

"Please." Tears stung my eyelids.

The woman took pity on me. "Take him over yonder—to the cabin by the edge of the woods. Maybe Granny Mawes can do somethin'."

With the last of my strength, I hauled Uncle Harry to the door of the ramshackle cabin she had directed me to. I knocked. No answer. I pounded on the door. "Please, I beg you... ." I was trying to get a better hold on Uncle Harry and move on, when the latch inside lifted and the door cracked open.

An old stooped woman poked her head out. She was under five feet tall. In the light flickering from a candle inside the cabin, her face was frightening.

"Miz... Mawes?"

The door pushed wider. "Nobody's called me that for a long time. Folks hereabout call me Granny." She smiled, and I could see her toothless gums.

"Can you help us?"

Granny Mawes studied my face—then looked at Uncle Harry

leaning against me. She hesitated so long I thought she was going to send us away. I tightened my arm around Uncle Harry's waist, ready to leave, when she flung the door back and motioned to me to come inside.

Surprisingly strong, she helped me lift Uncle Harry onto a crude wooden bed with a straw tick mattress in the corner of the room— then pulled some clean, worn cloths out of a cupboard. Limping to the fireplace, she lifted the kettle and filled a bowl with steaming water. Her hands shook as she removed the rag tied around Uncle Harry's head to examine the wound over his eye. She pressed the surrounding skin for swelling—then washed away the blackened grime and replaced the rag with a clean cloth. Uncle Harry groaned when she cut his tunic and pulled away the buckskin clinging to the wound in his shoulder.

"His head's all right, but that musket ball has to come out," she said.

The wound looked dark and angry. I moved closer to see better, and smelled the sick, sweet smell of gangrene. "The nearest surgeon's with Colonel Dunbar, eight miles away."

"This can't wait." Granny Mawes' blue eyes challenged me. "If you'll hold him, I'll see what I can do."

I looked at her gnarled fingers. Could she really cut out the musket ball with those hands? What if the knife slipped? What if she didn't know what she was doing?

Uncle Harry moaned—his face a deep red now. In the short time we had been there, he had started to pant. I didn't have any choice. If the musket ball didn't come out tonight, Uncle Harry would die!

CHAPTER FOURTEEN

THE LONG ROAD BACK

I woke up and couldn't remember where I was. Looking around the unfamiliar room, I was appalled by how poor the owner must be. Everything in the cabin had been broken and mended, from the few pieces of wooden furniture to the bit or two of crockery. But everything was spotlessly clean. Bunches of drying herbs hung from the ceiling, reminding me of home. An iron pot hanging from a hook simmered over a crackling fire. My mouth watered. Whatever was cooking smelled wonderful.

A snort from the bed where Uncle Harry lay brought me to my feet. My uncle wasn't awake, but the unhealthy flush that had worried me last night was gone. Last night! I shuddered, remembering. I had been afraid I wouldn't be able to hold Uncle Harry's thrashing body when Granny Mawes plunged the knife in his shoulder. Mercifully, Uncle Harry had fainted. He hadn't felt the pain when she dug deep into his flesh to pry the musket ball out of his shoulder—or felt the agony of the glowing iron she held to his gaping wound afterward.

"To purify it," she said, "and to stop the bleedin'." She concocted a sticky mess of something I couldn't identify, spread it on a clean rag, and bound it to Uncle Harry's burned flesh. "A poultice," she said, "—to draw out the poison."

My grim recollections were interrupted by the cabin door squeaking open.

"How's the patient this mornin'?" Granny Mawes hobbled to the bed, rested her crooked fingers on Uncle Harry's forehead, and nodded.

He stirred.

"Uncle Harry?"

"Josh?" He turned toward my voice. "Where am I? What am I doing here?"

"You were wounded."

"I remember that, but what…"

"We lost the battle. We're at Gist's Plantation. Granny Mawes here took a musket ball out of your shoulder." I motioned to her and then remembered that Uncle Harry couldn't see.

In a weak voice, he said, "Indebted to you, ma'am—and to you, Josh, for saving my life."

"We have to leave here this morning, Uncle Harry—if you're able. The army's pulling out at five o'clock."

He struggled to sit up.

"Not 'til you both have somethin' in your stomachs!" Granny Mawes brought out a couple of wooden trenchers and filled them with rabbit stew, the first food either of us had eaten since before the battle.

"How can I thank you?" I said later, from the doorway.

"I had a laddy like you once." Granny Mawes' eyes filled with tears. "Helpin' you has been a joy."

Gazing at her kindly face, I wondered how I had ever thought her frightening.

Provisions from Captain Dunbar had finally reached the plantation after midnight. The troops had broken their fast before dawn. They were falling into line, when Uncle Harry and I joined them. I had fretted about keeping up with the rest of the train, but with so few survivors—many of them sick and wounded—there was no need to worry. We covered the eight miles to Captain Dunbar's camp by afternoon.

His soldiers had prepared for the incoming wounded by clearing wagons of ammunition and provisions and burying them. A hundred wagons had been burned, for lack of horses to draw them.

The surgeons put the ailing to bed. Uncle Harry refused to be among them. "I'll be better off outside with you than inside a wagon in this murderous heat—if you can put up with me, Josh." He smiled for the first time, and I knew he was on the mend.

What was left of General Braddock's army began the long trek back to Fort Cumberland. When we came to ground, the surgeons changed the injured men's bandages. What with flies and the sweltering heat, many of the wounds crawled with maggots.

I nearly gagged at the sight and stench of the raw stumps and festering sores of the men being treated while Uncle Harry and I waited our turn. When the doctor finally got to us, he examined Uncle Harry's temple and eyes and bandaged them again. Nervous, I watched him pull the poultice from Uncle Harry's shoulder. Granny Mawes knew what she was doing! The wound was clean and already healing.

"You were lucky you were shot by a redcoat," the surgeon said.

"What do you mean, a redcoat?" Uncle Harry asked.

"This is a clean wound. The French use chewed balls that tear into the flesh and spread on impact." The doctor bound the wound and prepared to move on to the next man.

"Wait." I touched his arm. "What about his eyes?"

"The wounds are coming along. As to your uncle's sight, there's no way of telling. Keep his eyes bandaged. With time, perhaps they'll heal."

General Braddock died from his wounds at sunset. Next morning, before dawn, the army marched a short distance and halted to dig his grave in the middle of the road. I saw Mister Alton standing beside Captain Washington and waved to him. He came over to say hello.

"The chaplain is wounded," he said. "Frail as he is, the captain is going to conduct the service."

Squinting to see in the flickering torchlight, Captain Washington read a passage from the Bible, and General Braddock's blanket-covered body was buried.

Next morning, wagons began to wheel over the general's grave—followed by the marching troops. Uncle Harry explained that the reason they did that was to hide the whereabouts of the general's body so the Indians couldn't dig up his corpse and scalp him.

We marched ten miles that day. Uncle Harry suffered from a headache, but otherwise was stronger. With my hand to guide him, he had no trouble keeping up with the train.

That evening, after we made camp, I took out Oliver's fife. Looking at it, I wished I had told him the truth about who I was and where I had come from. Once we were friends, he would have forgiven me for lying. He wouldn't have cared that I wasn't perfect. I could see that now. My throat aching, I told Uncle Harry what Oliver had said before he died. He put his hand over his eyes when I came to the part about the shoes.

"It's rare to have such a friend, Josh."

With a heavy heart, I told Uncle Harry about Daniel. "When the first shots were fired, he just turned tail and ran!"

"Why would he do that, do you think?"

I thought about the things Daniel had said about the redcoats. From the beginning, he couldn't stand General Braddock. Every time the general did something he considered foolish, it made Daniel angry, and he didn't care who knew it.

"Dan'l said it was going to be a massacre."

"And he was right."

"Maybe it was just good sense, leaving the battle," I said, glad to come up with an excuse for Daniel that I could accept. "It sure didn't make him any hero."

"It didn't make him dead, either." Uncle Harry sighed. "He did what he thought he had to do. None of us are perfect, Josh."

I sure wasn't! I thought of all the lies I had told and the things I had done that had only caused trouble. My heart softened. "Dan'l didn't abandon me," I said. "He didn't want anything bad to happen to me, or he wouldn't have asked me to go with him. He was a true friend." But if I'd done what he wanted me to do, I wouldn't have been there when Uncle Harry needed me.

It took us almost two weeks to reach Fort Cumberland. When we arrived there, we made camp near Wills Creek. I left Uncle Harry resting in the shade of a mulberry tree and went to say my goodbyes.

In my mind's eye, I could see Oliver's lopsided grin welcome me as I approached our rock for the last time. I pulled out his fife and wobbled through a refrain of Greensleeves, imagining him laughing every time I missed a note. The thought that I'd never see him again made me want to cry. Death was so final.

I remembered when Grandmother Bedford had died. I thought I'd never get over it. Ma told me that sorrow heals with time. I wasn't sure it ever healed—but I had learned that it does get better.

I went to Captain Washington's tent. He looked pale and thin, writing in his journal. He must have heard me when I came in because he looked up and put down his quill. "So you're leaving us, Jed—or is it Josh?"

"Whichever you like, sir. I answer to both."

"I've been hearing good things about you from Mister Alton."

"Thank you, sir."

"Maybe our paths will cross again one day. Let us hope the circumstances are better."

I stood there, not sure how to approach him.

Finally he said, "Is there something I can do for you?"

"Yes, sir, if you please."

"Well speak up, lad, what do you want?'

I steeled myself to ask the favor. "My friend Oliver was killed..."

"I know." The captain's blue eyes that could look so cold seemed warm now. In a gentle voice, he said, "Go on."

"I promised him I'd send a letter to his sweetheart in Cork, if anything happened to him."

He gave me a searching look. "Would you like for me to write it?"

"Oh—no, sir. I know how to write. But I have no quill or

foolscap or any way to send it."

"I can take care of that." He gathered the things I needed together. Why don't you write it there?" He motioned to an empty chair beside his writing table.

I sat down and addressed the envelope—then chewed my lip, trying to think of a way to break the news that Oliver was dead. Picking up the quill again, I wrote:

Dear Tibby,

My friend Oliver Cunningham is dead. Killed by Indians. He died bravely. He wanted me to tell you that he loved you.
Your friend,

I hesitated—then signed the letter with my real name, placed it in the envelope, and handed it to Captain Washington.

"I'll post it, Jed—as soon as I reach Williamsburg."

"Thank you, sir."

Mister Alton stepped inside the tent just as I turned to leave. "Good luck, Jed. God be with you, son. If you ever come south, you know where I'll be."

I walked through Fort Cumberland, keenly aware of the changes since General Braddock's army had marched off to war. There was no more laughter... no more friendly talk. The fort was like an empty shell. The redcoats hadn't lived up to their boastful promises. In the two and a half months since I had left home, I felt as if I had aged ten years.

CHAPTER FIFTEEN

COMING TO TERMS

Just before dawn, while the air was still cool, I helped Uncle Harry get ready, and we began the long trek home. I was glad the campaign was over. War was more terrible than anything I could have imagined. But I wasn't sorry I ran away. If I hadn't, Oliver and I wouldn't have met.

Up to now, it had been easy to push most thoughts of home out of my mind. Tonight, I'd be back at the farm. Back to Ma and Sarah—my heart lifted at the thought of them—but also back to Pa and Matt. What would Pa say? What would he do to punish me, and how would I react?

A frog peeped in a tree nearby, reminding me of the time when Oliver asked if I had a sweetheart. What about Lettie? Did she know what I had done? Did she think I acted like a little boy, running away from home?

"You all right?" Uncle Harry asked. "Seem mighty quiet."

I didn't answer.

"It's going home, isn't it? You're afraid of what your pa's going to do."

"It's not only that. It's… everything."

Uncle Harry stumbled, and I clasped his arm more tightly.

"You were wrong to run away, Josh—but we've already been over that."

"I know."

"Fact is—you did it. Now you have to take the consequences like a man."

Walking along, I thought about some of the things that had happened since I left the farm. I'd let Buck wander off, but I'd saved Ranger from being stolen by deserters. I'd almost gotten Daniel and me killed by the bear—but I saved Half King's life when I killed the moccasin. With Willie's help, I had learned to apologize.

It was late afternoon when we reached the farm. "Hello, the cabin!" Uncle Harry called out.

The door was open to catch any breeze. Pa appeared in the doorway and stood there, looking at us. Ma stepped in the doorway beside him, saw who it was, and came running.

"Josh!" She threw her arms around me and held on tight.

"Joshie!" Sarah saw me and squealed—then toddled toward me.

I scooped her up, looking at Matt, who was now standing beside Pa. There was a look on my brother's face I couldn't read. He stepped outside, and someone else appeared in the doorway. Lettie! She smiled a big smile and nodded.

Pa moved then—came outside with the others. Ignoring me, he took Uncle Harry's arm and led him into the cabin.

"What're you doing here, Lettie?" I asked. Suddenly, the grimy clothes I had been wearing since the battle—that hadn't seemed all that important before—made me self-conscious. I smoothed my hair, wishing I had combed it.

"Papa came home and set everything right—and Mama was up and around in no time after you left." She looked away. "Matt came to our place three times, looking for you. He was worried as could be."

Matt worried about me? I didn't believe it.

"Matt said your ma was near crazy after you left," she said. "Mama said it'd be all right if I came and stayed awhile." She lowered her voice. "Your mother was really angry with your father when you ran away."

I followed the others inside. Ma turned and patted my cheek. "We'll talk later," she whispered.

She and Lettie went right to the cabinet and began pulling out leftovers while Pa helped Uncle Harry into a chair beside the table and began to ask him questions.

Matt sidled up to me. "We have a new cow, Josh."

I ignored him and stayed near the door, glad that Sarah was in my arms and I could put off having to say anything to Pa until I had a sense of things. How did he feel, having me home? Was he relieved to see me alive? Was he glad I wasn't wounded? Had his anger cooled? Ma kept turning and smiling at me while she prepared our meal, clearly happy that I was home and still in one piece.

Somehow, home didn't feel like home any more—although everything looked and smelled the same. Ma's spinning wheel stood in the corner, as always. Her summer herbs hung in fragrant bunches from the ceiling beside the fireplace. Looking at them, I was reminded of Granny Mawes. She had accepted me without any criticism and made me feel at home. Here, where I had spent my whole life, I felt like a stranger.

Matt was by the window, staring at my feet. "Where'd you get those funny shoes?"

I looked at Oliver's gift and didn't answer.

He walked over to Lettie and touched her arm as she set down a platter of sliced ham. "Thought we were going to take another walk together," he said, watching me.

Lettie stepped away. "Not now, Matt."

A jealous feeling knifed through my stomach. I focused on Sarah, pretending I hadn't heard. Lettie liked Matt now? She said he had come to visit three times. He wouldn't do that on my account! What was going on? I looked at Uncle Harry and began to listen to what he was saying.

"Our worst fears about the British came true." He picked at the bandage covering his eyes. "We lost five hundred men, James. Four hundred more were wounded."

131

"Terrible numbers," Pa agreed for once. "How many fought against you?"

"Some two hundred and fifty French and six hundred Indians."

"What were their losses?"

"Only sixteen French casualties," Uncle Harry said bitterly. "Twenty-seven of their Indians were wounded or killed."

"So few?" Pa shook his head in disbelief. He glanced in my direction, saw me listening, and leaned closer to Uncle Harry.

Pa didn't want to talk to me any more than I wanted to talk to him.

"Of three Virginia companies, only thirty men were left alive." Uncle Harry's mouth began to tremble, and he covered it with his hand. "Washington was the only mounted officer to escape injury."

I put Sarah in her highchair with her rag doll to play with and walked over to Ma. "I need a bath," I muttered, my voice low so Lettie couldn't hear.

"Now, Josh? Have something to eat, first."

"Now, Ma."

She looked at my clothes, stained with Oliver's blood in spite of all my efforts to wash it out once we reached Fort Cumberland. Handing Lettie the knife she had been using to cut cornbread, she took my hand. I was aware of Matt watching as she led me into the bedroom. She closed the door behind us and went to her trunk at the foot of the bed.

"Just look at how you've grown," she said. "I hope I've made these big enough." Opening the trunk, she pulled out some new breeches and a homespun shirt. "With every stitch, I told myself 'Josh will be home soon, and he'll be just fine.' I haven't finished the jacket yet."

She'd made me new clothes! I smoothed them with my hand. "Thank you, Ma. These are wonderful—but why?"

"Have you forgotten?"

"Forgotten what?" What was she talking about?

"I made these for your birthday." Her voice caught as she said, "What a grand surprise to have you come back on the very day!"

I scratched my head. "Today's my birthday?" I had completely forgotten.

She nodded and gave me a hug—then handed me a bar of lye soap and a fresh washcloth and towel. "You must be starved. Take a piece of cornbread with you. I'll save the rest of your supper for after your bath."

We walked back into the main room, my fine new clothes under my arm. I took a piece of cornbread off the platter Lettie was preparing and hurried outside.

The creek was about thirty yards behind the house. Downstream, there was a deep pocket where the water pooled. Wolfing down the cornbread, I made for it. Beside the water, I began to strip off my clothes. When I removed my shirt, I looked at my journal. What was I going to do with it? If Lettie liked Matt now... I sank down in the cool water and let the minnows nibble at my skin. The water felt wonderful. I scrubbed my body and scrubbed my hair, welcoming the sting of the lye.

It was dusk when I reached the cabin after bathing in the creek. I stepped inside, feeling refreshed.

The room hushed. I could see Matt eyeing my new clothes. Standing by the window in my mended breeches he looked pathetic, reminding me of Willie. His face looked peculiar. Why he was jealous! By running away from home and joining the campaign, I had stolen his dream. I'd always thought that. Now I knew it for sure. The revenge I had wanted so badly was complete.

I had expected to feel good about it. Instead, I just felt sorry for him. Before I could think it through and reconsider, I reached for my sling and pressed it in his hand.

Suddenly, the room closed in on me. I felt as if I couldn't breathe. I snatched the empty milk pail off its hook, made for the door, and ran to the barn. I could hear the rustling movement of a cow inside. Was her name Bessy, too? Were things going to be the same as when I left?

Seated on the milk stool inside the barn, I breathed in the familiar smells of hay and cow and soothed myself by milking. When I finished, I latched the barn door and set the pail of warm milk on the ground. Then I sat down and leaned against the barn's wooden siding to work out my plan.

A noise distracted me, and I looked up. Matt had followed me.

"Why did you do it, Matt?" I muttered. "Why did you let me take the blame for Bessy?"

"You remembered." He gave me a sour look. "I didn't want to get in trouble. Besides, you're Ma's favorite—always have been. Thought, if she was mad enough at you, she'd think better of me."

"If I'm Ma's favorite, it's because she lost my twin," I said. "And I can say the same thing about you and Pa. You're his favorite." A new thought occurred to me and nearly bowled me over. Matt had to be reliable, to stay in Pa's good graces. He couldn't afford to get in trouble. He must have felt just as trapped as I did!

He stood there, fiddling with my sling. "After you ran away, I told 'em."

"Told who—what?"

"After you left, I told the folks it was my fault that Bessy got out."

Surprised, I said, "How did they take it?"

"Ma was furious. Pa didn't say much." He threw the sling on the grass beside me and sat down. "I had to do all your chores."

"The milking, too?" I swiped my mouth with my hand to hide a smile.

He nodded and picked up the sling again. "I'm sorry for what I did."

"About me or about having to milk?"

We were quiet then. I spent the time counting fireflies. After a while, I stood up. "I'm leaving," I said.

"What?"

"I can't stay here. I'm leaving, first thing in the morning."

"Where will you go?"

"Amos Porter hires hands this time of year to help him bring in his crops."

For a minute, the Matt I loathed showed himself. "What makes you think he'd want to hire you?"

"Because I can do the job," I said, and I knew I could.

He stood up and stared at me. "You've changed."

I didn't answer at first. Things were better, but there was still no peace between us. I remembered how Oliver made peace with me after the fight, and I knew what I had to do.

"We don't like each other, Matt," I said. "Most of the time, we don't get along at all. But the thing is—we're family. Goldarnit, we're brothers! That counts for a lot." I held out my hand.

He hesitated—looked me in the eye—and shook it. Then he stuck my sling under his belt and sat down again. I could hear the yearning in his voice as he said, "Tell me about Fort Cumberland."

I sat down next to him and we had our first real conversation. I told him about Daniel and Captain Washington and what I had learned about the redcoats. I told him about Oliver and what good friends we'd been. Finally, I told him about the battle.

When I finished my story, we just sat there. The stars had come out, and a half-moon was rising. Matt rose to his feet. "C'mon, Josh. The folks'll be wondering what happened to us."

I picked up the pail of milk and we walked toward the cabin.

"Do you like Lettie?" he asked.

"Except for Oliver, we've been best friends forever. You know that."

"That's not what I mean. Do you love her?"

I thought about the journal inside my shirt. Then I thought about Oliver and how I'd lied to him about Lettie. "I believe I do love her, but I don't know if she feels that way about me." I stopped walking. "What about you, Matt? When I came home this afternoon you two looked thick as thieves."

He shrugged. "Lettie doesn't care a fig about me. I was just trying to make you jealous. Whenever we're alone, all she ever talks about is you."

CHAPTER SIXTEEN

HOME AT LAST

In the flickering candlelight the cabin seemed almost friendly when Matt and I walked in. Ma was standing beside Uncle Harry, her medicine box open on the table next to a trencher of food she had set out for my supper.

"This bandage is filthy," she murmured. She began to un-wrap Uncle Harry's head.

Nobody said anything, but the same thought was clearly on everyone's mind. Had his sight returned? I held my breath.

Ma lay the bandage aside. Uncle Harry touched his closed eyes lightly with his fingers. Then his eyes fluttered and slowly opened.

"Things are fuzzy, but I can see you, Josh!" he said, grinning.

We all started talking at once. Ma looked at me and then at Matt—studied our faces, and broke into a smile. "Have your supper, Josh, while Lettie and I serve the cake and punch. We have lots of things to celebrate!"

I sat down and began to eat. Cinder jumped in my lap and purred. We were all happy about Uncle Harry's eyes, and Ma was clearly delighted that Matt and I were on better terms. Lettie kept eyeing the two of us, looking puzzled. Other than that, it wasn't much of a celebration. The problem was—Pa still hadn't said a word to me, and everybody knew it. I kept sneaking looks at him through the corner of my eye.

Finally I yawned and said, "Thanks, Ma, for a nice birthday."
I pushed my chair away from the table and stood. "You have a houseful. I'll sleep in the barn."

"Me too," Matt said.

I turned to Uncle Harry. "Will you be all right?"

He smiled. "I'm fine. Ready for some shut-eye, myself. I'll come with you while you two get your things."

We said our goodnights, and the three of us walked to the ladder and climbed the rungs to the loft.

"You all right? " Uncle Harry asked, settling onto the pallet I had shared with Matt.

"I can't stay here, Uncle Harry. I think you know why."

He nodded. "I'm sorry about your Pa. Much as I admire him, he can be a stubborn so-and-so."

Matt and I gathered up what we needed and made our way to the barn. We spent most of the night just talking.

I wakened early next morning and milked Bessy Two while Matt watched. Sure enough, that was the new cow's name. We were on the way to the cabin when Lettie appeared on the path ahead.

Matt reached for the pail of milk and took it from me. "You need to talk."

As soon as Lettie reached me, she said, "I want to apologize for the way I acted when you came to the plantation... the flower and all. Don't know what got into me."

The rose—dry now and still pressed between the pages of my journal. I took her hand and led her to a grassy spot under a maple tree. We sat down. I reached inside my shirt for my journal and handed it to her.

"This is for you, Lettie."

She ran her fingers over the smooth leather and opened it. "Oh, Josh." She picked up the rose and smelled it—then cradled it in her hand and began to read.

I turned away, feeling self-conscious.

She read the first page and clasped the journal to her. "I'll treasure this forever," she said. "I'll save the rest of it for later, when I'm alone."

"Oliver had a sweetheart, Lettie."

She gave me a searching look. "Does this mean we're sweethearts, Josh?"

She looked so pretty, sitting there in her blue dress. "What about Matt?"

"Oh, Josh, you know better."

Her eyes were bluer than ever as she lifted her lips for my kiss.

"We'd better get back to the cabin," she said, touching my cheek.

"I'm not going to stay here, Lettie. I'm not like I was before I left home."

"What will you do?"

I told her my plan to ask Amos Porter for a job.

"Wish you could come home with me," she said.

I grinned and shook my head. "That's all your folks need—another boy around."

She giggled.

Hand in hand, we walked up the path—then paused by the cabin's open door. Ma was at the stove, stirring something. The others were sitting around the table—Sarah in her highchair next to Matt, her mouth smeared with the porridge she was feeding herself. "If it hadn't been for Josh, I wouldn't be sitting here now," Uncle Harry said.

"C'mon." Lettie pulled me inside.

Ma had fixed us a fine breakfast of ham and eggs and toasted bread with honey. The honey reminded me of Oliver and Willie, and I lost my appetite. I made myself sit there.

For the first time since I came home, I caught Pa looking at me a couple of times. But he still didn't say anything. As soon as I could, I excused myself and climbed the ladder to the loft. I could hear their voices down below. They were talking about me. Then I heard Matt climb the ladder—or so I thought.

"Matt says you're leaving us," Pa said.

I nodded. "This time, I'm not running away."

He cleared his throat. "Your ma near killed me when you ran away. She blamed me for it."

He watched me gather my clothes together and place them on a piece of canvas. I couldn't look at him.

He cleared his throat again. "Maybe I have been a little hard on you."

I picked up a piece of rope and looped it around my things, making a bundle. "I think I understand why now," I said, concentrating on what I was doing. "You couldn't depend on me." But couldn't you show me you loved me anyhow, Pa? I couldn't say the words.

"Being reliable is one thing. But a man is only as good as his word, Josh—and you've been careless with the truth, too."

What he said hurt me, but I knew he was right. Setting the bundle aside, I said, "I don't lie any more."

Pa gave me a long look. "Harry told me some mighty fine things about you." He hesitated. "By golly, son—you've made me proud!"

My breath caught. He said it! He called me son! I couldn't believe my ears.

For the first time I could remember, Pa opened his arms to me.

END NOTE

The killing of Coulon de Jumonville, the young ensign sent to Great Meadows to present George Washington with the summons asking him to leave what they considered to be French territory, was the spark that ignited the Seven Years War—a war that would decide whether America would be ruled by England or by France.

England won the Seven Years War, but seeds of yearning for American independence had been sown: What came to be known as the Battle of the Monongahela convinced the colonists that the British were not invincible and they might very well do without them.

As a result of George Washington's courageous actions on the battlefield, Governor Robert Dinwiddie appointed him commander of all Virginia troops a month after the defeat at Fort Duquesne. Twenty years later, at the onset of the War for Independence, Washington was named commander-in-chief of military forces in the colonies. By that time, Thomas Gage was commander-in-chief of British forces in North America. The former comrades-in-arms were now enemies.

John Finley and a group of hunters explored the land west of the Alleghenies, the first white men to do so. Inspired by his friend's glowing accounts of the bountiful game and richness of the land, Daniel Boone returned there with him. In 1775, Boone helped blaze a trail through the Cumberland Gap—which led to the development of the first white settlements in Kentucky.

CPSIA information can be obtained at www.ICGtesting.com
Printed in the USA
BVOW08s0816221013

334159BV00001B/2/P

9 780979 939549